'Its symbolist exploration of young love… is endearingly eccentric'

The Times

'Cracked geodes. Circular waterfalls. Eskimos on sleds crossing polar seas. An extraordinary visual experience in the form of an impossible love story that consistently defies its own description. A meditation on beauty told through a fascination with form'

Frieze

'What a brave man she was, and what a good woman'

Ivan Turgenev

'Her voice can be intimate, unpretentious, gentle, sympathetic, and disarmingly honest'

New York Times

GEORGE SAND was born Amandine-Aurore Lucile Dupin in Paris in 1804 and brought up at Nohant, her grandmother's country home. In 1822 Sand married Baron Casimir Dudevant but left him and their disastrous marriage to seek a better life in Paris. Her most famous novels portray the struggles of women against social constraints, especially marriage. Legendary for her numerous love affairs with such prominent figures as Prosper Mérimée, Alfred de Musset and Frédéric Chopin, Sand was also a celebrated writer whose works influenced Dostoevsky, Tolstoy, Flaubert and Proust.

GEORGE SAND

LAURA: A JOURNEY INTO THE CRYSTAL

Translated from the French by
Sue Dyson

PUSHKIN PRESS
LONDON

Pushkin Press
71–75 Shelton Street
London, WC2H 9JQ

Laura: A Journey into the Crystal was first published as
Laura, Voyage dans le Cristal in France, 1864

First published by Pushkin Press in 2004
This edition first published by Pushkin Press in 2018

3 5 7 9 8 6 4 2

ISBN 13: 978 1 78227 414 8

Offset by Tetragon, London
Printed and bound by CPI Group (UK) Ltd, Croydon, CRO 4YY

www.pushkinpress.com

LAURA:
A JOURNEY
INTO THE
CRYSTAL

My dearest daughter,

I dedicate this fable to you, that it may remind you of the discourses given to us by your husband while we ourselves marvelled at the beauty of the mineralogical specimen instead of following exclusively its geological formation. In several years' time, your son, who now has more beautiful dreams in his crib than I in my inkwell, will read this story, and he will take from it, perhaps, a taste for research or some serious theory. For those disposed to knowing and understanding it need not be more. For children, and many grown ups, this is the sole practical purpose of such a fiction.

Nohant, 1 December 1863

I

WHEN I MET M. HARTZ, he was a naturalist and dealer who ran his business affairs in a quiet way, selling minerals, insects or plants to collectors. Entrusted with an errand for him, I had been taking little interest in the precious objects which cluttered his shop when, while chatting to him about the mutual friend who had put us in touch, and mechanically touching an egg-shaped stone which lay within my reach, I dropped it. It split into two almost equal halves, which I hastened to pick up, begging the shopkeeper to forgive my clumsiness.

Do not distress yourself, he replied kindly; it was destined to be broken with a blow from a hammer. It is a geode of no great value and, moreover, isn't everyone curious to see the inside of a geode?

I do not know exactly what a geode is, I told him, and I have no desire to know.

Why? he asked; are you not an artist?

Yes, I try to be; but the critics do not want artists giving the impression that they know anything outside their art, and the public do not like the artist to appear to know any more than they do about anything at all.

I think the public, the critic and yourself are all mistaken. The artist was born to be a traveller; everything is a journey for his spirit, and without leaving his fireside or the shady spots in his garden, he is entitled to range over all the highways and byways of the world. Give him anything to read or look at, be it a lively study or dry as dust; he will be passionate about anything that is new to him.

He will naively be astonished not to have yet lived like that, and he can translate the pleasure of his discovery into any form at all, without ceasing to be himself. The artist is no better able to choose his type of life and the nature of his impressions than are other human beings. From outside, he receives sun and rain, shadow and light, like everyone else. Do not ask him to create beyond the confines of what strikes him. He is subject to the action of the surroundings he passes through, and it is very good that it is so, for were that action to cease he would be extinguished and become sterile. So, went on M. Hartz, you have a perfect right to educate yourself, if it entertains you and if the opportunity presents itself. There is no danger therein for anyone who is truly an artist.

In the same way that a true scholar can be an artist, if this excursion into the realm of art does not harm his serious studies?

Yes, replied the honest shopkeeper; the entire question is to be something determinate and somewhat solid in one direction or the other. That, I agree, is not given to everyone! And, he added with a kind of sigh, if you doubt yourself, do not look too long at that geode.

Is it some stone with a magical influence?

All stones have that influence, but above all geodes, in my opinion.

You have aroused my curiosity ... So, what do you mean by "geode"?

In mineralogy, a "geode" means any hollow stone whose interior is lined with crystals or incrustations; and any mineral whose interior contains voids or little caverns, which you can see in this one, is called a geodic stone.

He gave me a magnifying glass, and I saw that these voids did indeed look like mysterious grottoes furnished with stalactites of extraordinary brilliance; then, considering the geode as a whole and several others which the shopkeeper handed me, I saw peculiarities of shape and colour which, enlarged by the imagination, constituted Alpine areas, deep ravines, grandiose mountains, glaciers, everything that makes up an imposing, sublime natural tableau.

Everyone has noticed this, I said to M. Hartz; a hundred times in my mind, I myself have compared the pebble I picked up at my feet to the mountain looming up above my head, and found that the specimen was a sort of summary of the mass; but, today, I am more powerfully struck by it than before, and these choice crystals you show me put me in mind of a fantastical world where all is transparency and crystallisation. It is not a matter of confusion or vague bedazzlement, as I imagined when reading those fairytales in which people explore diamond palaces. I see here that nature works better than fairies. These transparent bodies are grouped in such a way as to produce slender shadows, smooth reflections, and the fusion of shades does not prevent the composition from being logical and harmonious. Truly, this enchants me and makes me eager to look in your shop.

No, said M. Hartz, taking the rock specimens from my hands, you must not travel that road too quickly: you see here a man who was almost a victim of the crystal!

A victim of the crystal? What a strange conjunction of words!

It is because in those days I was neither yet learned nor

11

an artist that I encountered the danger ... But it would be too long a story, and you do not have the time to listen to it.

No sooner said than done, I cried out, I adore stories whose titles I do not understand. I have all the time in the world, tell it to me!

I would tell it very badly, replied the shopkeeper, but I wrote it down in my youth.

And, extracting a yellowed manuscript from the depths of a drawer, he read me the following:

I was nineteen years old when I was appointed assistant to the deputy-assistant curator of the natural history institute, mineralogy section, in the learned and famous town of Fischausen, in Fischemburg. My office, which was entirely pointless, had been created for me by one of my uncles, the director of the establishment, in the judicious hope that, having absolutely nothing to do there, I would be in my element and could wondrously develop the remarkable aptitude I had demonstrated for utter idleness.

My first exploration of the long gallery containing the collection produced in me only a frightful sinking feeling. What! I was going to live here, in the midst of these inert things, in company with these innumerable pebbles of every shape, size and colour, all as dumb as each other, and all labelled with barbarous names, of which I promised myself never to remember a single one!

My pleasant existence had been no more than truancy in the most literal meaning of the word, and my uncle, who had noticed the shrewdness with which, from early childhood, I had found the wild blackberries and green dwarf apple trees behind fences, and the patience with which I had ferreted around in the hedge before pouncing on the nests of thrushes and linnets, had flattered himself that sooner or later he would see the instincts of a serious nature-lover awaken in me; but, as subsequently I had been the most able gymnast at school when it came to scaling a wall and escaping, my uncle wanted to punish me a little by shutting me away in the austere contemplation of the globe's bones, making me, moreover, regard the study of plants and animals as future compensation.

What a long way it was, from this dead world to which I was consigned, to the aimless and nameless delights of my wanderings! I spent several weeks seated in a corner, as gloomy as the columns of prismatic basalt which made up the monument's peristyle, as sad as the bench made from fossilised oysters, at which I saw my patrons cast glances filled with fatherly affection.

Each day, I listened to lectures; that is, a series of words that furnished me with no meaning and which returned to me in dreams like cabbalistic incantations; or else I attended geology classes given by my worthy uncle. The dear man would not have lacked for eloquence, had ungrateful nature not afflicted its most fervent adorer with an insurmountable stammer. His well-meaning colleagues assured him that his lecture was all the more valuable, and that his infirmity had the useful feature of exercising a mnemotechnic influence on the audience, who were enchanted to hear the principal syllables of the words repeated several times over.

As for me, I escaped the benefits of this method by regularly falling asleep as soon as each session began. From time to time, a sharp explosion of the old man's halting voice would make me leap up on my bench; I would half-open my eyes and, through the clouds of my lethargy, would spot his bald pate, gleaming in the light from a stray May sunbeam, or his hand, cupping a fragment of rock which he seemed to want to throw at my head. I quickly closed my eyes again and went back to sleep on these consoling words: "This, gentlemen, is a well-determined specimen of the material which forms the subject of this lesson. The chemical analysis gives, etc."

Sometimes, a neighbour with a cold would also catch me unawares by blowing his nose with a trumpeting sound. Then I would see my uncle drawing the outlines of geological events in chalk on the enormous blackboard behind him. He turned his back to the audience, and the oversized collar of his suit, cut in the *directoire* style, pushed up his ears in the strangest way. Then, everything would become confused in my brain, the corners of his drawing with those of his person, and I came to see in him nothing but insane straightenings-out and discordant stratifications. I had strange fantasies bordering on hallucination. One day, when he was giving us a lecture on volcanoes, I imagined I could see, in the gaping mouths of certain old adepts who were arranged around him, an equal number of little craters about to erupt, and to me the sound of the applause appeared to be the signal for those subterranean detonations which throw out blazing stones and vomit incandescent lava.

My Uncle Tungstenius (the *nom de guerre* which had replaced his family name) was rather malicious beneath his apparent bonhomie. He had sworn that he would get to the bottom of my resistance, whilst appearing not to have noticed it. One day, he came up with the idea of making me undergo a formidable ordeal, which was to place me once again in the presence of my cousin Laura.

Laura was the daughter of my Aunt Gertrude, sister of my late father, who was Tungstenius' younger brother. Laura was an orphan, although her father was alive. He was an active trader who, following some second-rate business affairs, had left for Italy, from where he had passed into Turkey. There, it was said, he had found the means to make himself wealthy; but you were never sure of anything with him. He wrote very little, and reappeared at such rare intervals, that we scarcely knew him. On the other hand, his daughter and I had known each other a great deal, for we had been brought up together in the country; then the time had come to separate us and send us to boarding school and we had forgotten each other, or very nearly.

I had left a thin, yellow child; now I found a girl of sixteen, slender, rose-pink, with magnificent hair, azure eyes, a smile filled with the incomparable graces of gaiety and goodness. I don't know if she was pretty; she was delectable and my surprise was so dazzling that it plunged me into the most complete idiocy.

Now then, Cousin Alexis, she said to me, what are you doing, and how do you spend your time here?

I dearly wish I could have found an answer other than the one I gave her; but for all my searching and stammering, I had to confess that I spent my time doing nothing.

What! she exclaimed with deep astonishment, nothing? Is it possible to live without doing anything, unless one is ill? Are you ill then, my poor Alexis? And yet you don't look as if you are.

I had to confess once again that I was perfectly well.

Then, she said, touching my forehead with her sweet little finger, which wore a pretty ring of white cornelian, your sickness is here: you are bored in town.

That is the truth, Laura, I cried out fervently; I miss the countryside and the time when we were so happy together.

I was proud to have at last found such a fine retort; but the peal of laughter that greeted it sent a mountain of confusion tumbling down upon my heart.

I believe you are mad, said Laura. You may miss the countryside, but not the happiness we savoured together; for we always went our own ways, you pillaging, picking, spoiling everything, and me making little gardens where I loved to see things germinate, grow green and blossom. The countryside was a paradise for me, because I love it for its own sake; as for you, it is your freedom for which you weep, and I feel sorry for you, not knowing how to occupy yourself as a consolation. This proves that you understand nothing of the beauty of nature, and that you are not worthy of freedom.

I do not know if Laura was repeating a phrase composed by our uncle and learned by heart; but she reeled it off so well that I was crushed. I fled, hid myself in a corner, and dissolved into tears.

In the days that followed, Laura did not speak to me again except to say hello and goodnight, and I was stunned to hear her talking about me in Italian with her governess. As they were constantly looking at me, it clearly did concern my poor self; but what were they saying? Sometimes it seemed to me that one of them spoke of me with contempt, and the other defended me with an air of compassion. However, as they often changed roles, it was impossible for me to know which of them really did feel sorry for me and sought to make excuses for me.

I remained living with my uncle, that is to say in a part of the establishment where he had assigned me a little pavilion, separated from the one he lived in by the botanical gardens. Laura spent her holidays with him, and I saw her at meal times. I found her always busy, either reading, embroidering, painting flowers or making music. I saw clearly that she was never bored; but I dared not speak to her again and ask her the secret of taking pleasure in any and every occupation.

At the end of a fortnight, she left Fischausen for Fischerburg, where she was to stay with her governess and an elderly female cousin who took the place of her mother. I had not dared break the ice; but the blow had hit home, and I set to studying ardently, without arguing, examining, selecting or reasoning, every element of the programme devised by Uncle Tungstenius.

Was I in love? I did not know, and even today I am still not certain. My self-esteem had been cruelly wounded for the first time. Until then impervious to my uncle's silent disdain and my fellow-disciples' teasing, I had blushed at Laura's pity. All the others were drivellers as far as I was concerned, she alone had seemed to exercise a right in criticising me.

One year later, I was completely transformed. Was it to my advantage? Those around me said so, and—aided by my vanity—I had a very good opinion of myself. There was not one word of my uncle's lesson that I could not have slotted into its place in the sentence it belonged to, not one sample in the lithological collection which I could not have designated by its name, along with that of its group, its variety, and the whole analysis of its composition, the entire history of its formation and its deposit. I even knew the name of the donor of each precious item, and the date when that item had entered the gallery.

Among these latter names was one that appeared many times in our catalogues, and particularly with regard to the most beautiful gemstones. It was that of Nasias, a name unknown in the field of study, and which rather intrigued me on account of its mysterious strangeness. My comrades knew no more on the subject than I. According to some, this man Nasias was an Armenian Jew who had formerly made exchanges between our exhibition hall and other collections of the same type. Others said it was the pseudonym of a disinterested donor. My uncle did not seem to know any more about him than we did. The date of his dispatches went back around a hundred years.

Laura came back with her governess for the holidays. I was once again presented to her with glowing compliments on my account from my uncle. I held myself straight as a stone pillar, and looked at Laura confidently. I was expecting to see her a little confused at the sight of my merit. Alas! she was nothing of the kind. The little imp began to laugh, took my hand and, holding on to it, looked me up and down with an air of teasing admiration; after which, she declared to our uncle that she found me much uglier.

However, I did not become disconcerted and, thinking that she still doubted my abilities, I set to questioning my uncle on a point which I felt he had neglected in his last lecture, an ingenious pretext for treating the ladies to a display of technical words and theories I had learned by heart. My uncle lent himself with an obliging lack of pretentiousness to this stratagem, which lasted some considerable time and showed off all my talents.

Laura did not appear to pay it any attention, and at the far end of the table she began a hushed conversation in Italian with her governess. I had studied this language a little in my brief leisure moments; I lent an ear several times, and recognised that they were having a discussion on the way to preserve green peas then, in my own eyes I regained the upper hand. Although Laura had grown yet more beautiful, I felt indifferent to her charms, and I left her saying to myself: "If I had known that you were only a silly little middle-class girl, I would not have taken so much trouble to show you of what I am capable."

Despite this reaction on the part of my self-pride, after an hour had passed I felt very sad, and as though I were being crushed by the weight of an immense disappointment. My immediate superior, the deputy assistant curator, saw me sitting in the corner of the gallery, looking shattered and with the gloomy expression I had habitually worn the previous year.

What is wrong? he asked me. Anyone would think that today you are remembering having been the greatest slowcoach in all creation.

Walter was an excellent young man: twenty-four years old, with an amiable face, a serious mind and a cheerful demeanour. His eyes and voice were imbued with the serenity of a clear conscience. He had always shown indulgence and affection towards me. I could not open my heart to him, for I could not see clearly into it myself; but I let him see the preoccupations which were rising up vaguely within me, and in the end I asked him what he thought of our arid studies, which had value only in the eyes of a few scientific adepts and remained a closed book to common mortals.

My dear boy, he replied, there are three ways of viewing our studies' goal. Your uncle, who is a respectable scholar, sits astride just one of these ways, and the pony he is riding with such panache, the one he spurs on furiously, and which often carries him away beyond all certainty, is called hypothesis. The rough, ardent horseman wishes, like Curtius, to plunge into the abysses of the earth, but there to discover the beginning of things and the successive and regular development of those first things. I believe he is seeking the impossible: chaos will not let go of its prey, and the word mystery is written on the cradle of earthly life. It matters not, your uncle's works have great value, because in the midst of many errors, he unearths many truths. Without the hypothesis which fascinates him and which has fascinated so many others, we would still find ourselves limited to the inexact symbolism of Genesis.

"But," Walter continued, "there is a second way of viewing science, and this is the one that has won me over. It consists of applying to industry the riches which slumber between the leaves of the earth's bark and which, every day, thanks to the progress of physics and chemistry, reveal to us new peculiarities and elements of well-being, sources of infinite power for the future of human societies.

"As for the third way, it is interesting but puerile. It consists of knowing the detail of the innumerable events and minute modifications that the mineralogical elements present. This is the science of details, which lovers of collections possess and which also interests lapidaries, jewellers . . ."

And women! I cried out with an accent of disdainful pity as I saw my cousin, who had just entered the gallery, walking slowly along the glass cabinet that contained the gemstones.

She heard my exclamation, turned round, threw me a look that embodied the most complete indifference, and calmly continued her examination without paying me any further attention.

I was going to continue the conversation with Walter, when he enquired if I was not going to offer my arm to my cousin and give her the explanations she might desire.

No, I replied, loudly enough to be heard. My cousin has seen her uncle's collection many times before, and the only thing that might interest her here, is precisely the one that interests us very little.

I confess, Walter went on, lowering his voice and showing me the side of the gallery which Laura was walking along, that I would give all the precious, priceless stones heaped up in those glass cases for the beautiful specimens of iron and coal which lie here, close to us. The miner's pick, my friend, there you have the symbol of the world's future, and as for these glittering trifles that decorate the heads of queens or the arms of courtesans, I care as much about them as about a wisp of straw. The work on a grand scale, my dear Alexis, the work which benefits everyone and which projects the rays of civilisation far into the distance, that is what dominates my thoughts and directs my studies. As for hypothesis . . .

What are you saying about hypo . . . po . . . pothesis? the annoyed voice of my Uncle Tungstenius stammered behind us. Hypo . . . po . . . pothesis is a term of derision used by l . . . l . . . lazy people who receive their opinions ready-made and dismiss the investigations of great minds as if they were chimeras.

Then, little by little growing calmer in the face of Walter's apologies and denials, the fellow went on without stuttering too much:

You will do well, children, never to abandon the governing thread of logic. There are no effects without a cause. The earth, the sky, the universe, and we ourselves, are only effects, the results of a sublime or fatal cause. Study the effects, by all means, but not without seeking the essential reason why nature itself exists.

"You are right, Walter, not to absorb yourself in the minutiae of purely mineralogical classifications and denominations; but you seek the useful with as much narrowness of thought as the mineralogists seek the rare. I care no more than you for diamonds and emeralds, which are the pride and amusement of a small number of people who are privileged to be wealthy; but, when you lock your entire soul away within the walls of some middlingly rich mine, you bring to my mind the mole who flees from the sun's rays.

"The sun of intelligence, my child, is reasoning.

Induction and deduction, there is no way out of that, and it matters little to me that you take me round the whole world in a steamship, if you never teach me why the earth is a globe and why this globe has evolutions and revolutions. Learn to strike iron, to convert it into cast iron or steel, I consent to that; but, if your whole life is nothing but an application to material things, you might just as well be iron yourself, in other words an inert substance deprived of reasoning. Man does not live by bread alone, my friend; he does not live completely except by the development of his faculties of examination and comprehension."

My uncle went on in this vein for some time, and, without allowing himself to contradict him, Walter defended as best he could the theory of the direct utility of the treasures of science. According to him, man could not arrive at the illumination of the mind until he had conquered the joys of the positive life.

I listened to this interesting discussion, whose scope struck me for the first time. I had got to my feet and, leaning on a copper rail which protects the glass cases from the outside, I gazed mechanically towards the mineralogical collection which Laura had examined a moment before, and which had been disdained in unison by my uncle, by Walter and by myself. I had moved to stand there without quite knowing why, for my uncle and Walter had turned towards the rocks, that is the purely geological collection. Perhaps, without my realising it, I was dominated by the vague pleasure of breathing in the scent of a white rose that Laura had placed and forgotten on the edge of the glass case.

Whatever the reason, my eyes were fixed on the series of quartz hyalines, also called rock crystals, before which Laura had appeared to halt for a moment with a certain pleasure, and, whilst listening to my uncle's reasoning, and wishing to forget Laura, who had disappeared, I contemplated a magnificent geode of amethyst quartz, completely filled with crystals which were truly remarkable, transparent and had the freshness of prisms.

However, my thoughts were not as fixed as my gaze; they floated at random, and the scent of the little musk rose brought my being back under the control of instinct. I loved that rose, and yet I believed I hated the one who had plucked it. I breathed in its scent with aspirations that translated themselves into kisses, I pressed it to my lips with a disdain that translated itself into bites. Suddenly I felt a light hand upon my shoulder, and a delicious voice, the voice of Laura, spoke in my ear.

Do not turn round, do not look at me, she said; leave that poor rose alone, and come with me to gather the flowers of stone that do not wither. Come, follow me. Do not listen to my uncle's cold reasoning and Walter's blasphemies. Quickly, quickly, friend, let us leave for the fairy regions of the crystal. I am running towards them, follow me, if you love me!

I felt so surprised and troubled, that I had the strength neither to look at Laura, nor to answer her. Moreover, she was already no longer at my side; she was in front of me, as if she had passed through the glass case, or the case had become an open door. She was fleeing or rather flying in a luminous space, and I followed her, not knowing where I was, nor by what fantastical brightness I was dazzled.

Fatigue halted me and overcame me after a period of time whose length I could not calculate. Discouraged, I let myself fall. My cousin had disappeared.

Laura! dear Laura! I cried out in despair, where have you led me, and why have you abandoned me?

I then sensed Laura's hand upon my shoulder once more, and her voice speaking in my ear again. At the same time, far away Uncle Tungstenius's piercing voice was saying:

No, there is no hypo . . . po . . . pothesis in all of that!

However Laura was speaking to me as well, and I could not understand her. I thought at first that it was in Italian, then in Greek, and finally I recognised that it was in a completely new language, which little by little was revealing itself to me like the memory of another life. I grasped the meaning of the last sentence very clearly.

So, see where I have brought you, she was saying, and understand that I have opened your eyes to the sky's light.

I then began to see and understand in what surprising place I found myself. I was with Laura in the centre of the amethyst geode which graced the glass case in the mineralogical gallery; but what up to then I had taken blindly and on the faith of others for a block of hollow flint, the size of a melon cut in half and lined inside with prismatic crystals of irregular size and groupings, was in reality a ring of tall mountains enclosing an immense basin filled with steep hills bristling with needles of violet quartz, the smallest of which might have exceeded the dome of St Peter's in Rome both in volume and in height.

From that moment on I was no longer astonished by the tiredness I had experienced while running up one of these rocky needles, and I felt a great surge of fear as I saw that I was on the slope of a sparkling precipice, at the bottom of which mysterious shimmers were calling to me with a vertiginous fascination.

Stand up and fear nothing, Laura told me; in this land, thoughts walk and the feet follow. Those who understand cannot fall.

Tranquil, Laura was indeed walking on these steep slopes, which plunged down in all directions towards the abyss, and whose polished surface received the full brilliance of the sun and reflected it back in iridescent sprays. The place was admirable, and I soon saw that I could walk there as safely as Laura. Finally she sat down on the edge of a small crack and asked me with a childish laugh if I recognised the place.

How could I recognise it? I said. Is this not the first time I have come here?

Silly-head! she replied, have you already forgotten that, last year, you handled the geode clumsily and dropped it on the gallery floor? One of the crystals was chipped, you didn't make a great fuss about it; but the trace of the accident has remained, and here it is. You have looked at it often enough to recognise it. Today, it serves you as a cave to shelter your poor head, tired out by the brilliance of the sun on the gemstone.

Indeed, Laura, I replied, I now recognise it very well; but I cannot understand how a break barely visible to the naked eye, in a specimen which my two hands could contain, has become a cavern in which the two of us can sit down on the flank of a mountain which could cover our entire town . . .

And, Laura went on, at the centre of a land that embraces a horizon whose depths your gaze can barely grasp? All this astonishes you, my poor Alexis, because you are a child without experience and without contemplation. Take a good look at this charming land, and you will easily understand the transformation that the geode seems to have effected upon you.

I gazed for a long time, and without tiring, at the dazzling vista we overlooked. The more I looked at it, the more able I became to bear its brilliance, and little by little it became as gentle upon my eyes as the greenery of the woods and meadows of our earthly regions. I was surprised to discern in it general shapes reminiscent of our glaciers, and soon even the smallest details of this gigantic crystallisation became as familiar to me as if I had explored them a hundred times in every direction.

You see, my companion then said, picking up one of the brilliant stones which lay beneath our feet, you see, this circular, hollow mountain range is just like this pebble, with its empty centre. One may be small and the other immense, but the difference is scarcely appreciable in the limitless expanse of creation. Each jewel in this vast screen has its own matchless value, and the mind which in its love cannot associate the grain of sand with the star is a sick mind, or played false by the deceptive notion of reality.

Was it Laura who spoke to me in this way? I sought to verify this; but she too shone like the brightest of the gemstones, and my eyes, by now accustomed to the splendours of the new world she had revealed to me, could not bear the additional radiance which seemed to emanate from her.

My dear Laura, I said, I am beginning to understand. And yet up there, a long way from here, and all around the horizon which encloses us, there are icy peaks and snowfields . . .

Look at the little geode, said Laura, placing it in my hand; you can clearly see that the crystals around the perimeter are limpid like ice and veined with opaque shades of white, like snow. Come with me, and you shall see at close quarters these eternal glaciers where cold is unknown and where death cannot seize us unawares.

I followed her, and this journey—which I estimated must have been of several leagues—was covered so swiftly that I was unaware of the moments passing. We were soon on the tallest summit of the great ice peak, which was in reality just a colossal prism of milky hyaline quartz, as was borne out, on a manageably small scale, by the geode which I held as a point of comparison, and just as Laura had declared to me; but what a grandiose sight came into view again from the very summit of the great white crystal! At our feet, the circle of amethyst, drowned in its own reflections, was now only a small element of the picture, agreeable because of the melancholy sweetness of its lilac tints, the elegance of its shapes contributing to the harmony of the whole. How many other splendours were unfurled in space!

O Laura, my dear Laura! I cried out, bless you for bringing me here! Where did you learn of the existence of these marvels, and how to reach them?

What does that matter to you! she replied; gaze upon the beauty of the crystalline world and savour it. The valley of the amethyst is, as you can see, only one of the

28

thousand aspects of this nature, whose riches are inexhaustible. Here, on the other side of the large crystal, you see the charming world of the jaspers with their changing veins. No cataclysm has sullied these magnificent, patient works of nature, or buried them in barbaric mixtures and brutal confusions. Whilst in our little world, troubled and refashioned a hundred times, the gemstone is shattered, dispersed, enshrouded in a thousand unknown, dark places, here it is plain for all to see. It sparkles, reigns everywhere, fresh and pure, and truly royal as it was in the first days of its happy formation.

"Further off, you can see the valleys where amber-coloured chalcedony is rounded into powerful hills, while a chain of dark, glowing-red zirconium completes the illusion of a limitless blaze. The lake which half-reflects them at its edges, but whose centre presents a surface of slackly lapping waves, is made up of indeterminate shades of chalcedony, whose nebulous fleeciness reminds one of white horses on the sea when there is a steady breeze.

"As for these masses of beryls and sapphires, a material whose rarity is so prized among us, they have no more importance here than God's other works. They stretch out to infinity in slender colonnades which you take perhaps for far-off forests, as I wager you take those slender, tender stems of green chalcedony to be thickets, and those crystalline efflorescences of pyromorphite for carpets of velvety moss caressing the edges of the many-coloured agate ravine; but that is nothing.

"Let us go on a little, you shall explore the opal oceans where the sun, that blazing diamond whose creative power is unknown to me, plays in all the reflections of the rainbow. Do not linger on these islands of turquoise, further on are those of tender lazulite and of lapis, run through with veins of gold.

"Here is mad labradorite, the reflections from its facets by turns colourless and pearly, and aventurine with silver rain that displays its polished flanks, while the fires of red, warm almandine, whose praises were once sung by a seer called Hoffmann, are concentrated around the centre of its austere mountain.

"As for me, I love those humble rose gypsums forming long walls, piled on top of each other, right up to the skies, and those fluorites lightly tinted with the freshest colours, or then again those blocks of feldspar, which we call moonstone, because it has the smooth reflection of that heavenly body's rays.

"If you will climb to the poles of this enchanted world, across the ice floes of satiny sericolite and limpid aquamarine, we shall see the permanent aurora borealis which man has never gazed upon, and you will understand that, in this universe which you see as immobile, the most intense life palpitates in the breaths of an energy so formidable that . . ."

Here, my cousin Laura's intoxicating voice was drowned out by a din like that of a hundred million thunderclaps. A hundred billion resplendent fireworks shot up into a black sky which I had at first taken for a measureless vault of tourmaline, but which was torn into a hundred billion burning strips. All the reflections were extinguished, and I saw, laid bare, the heaven's abysses scattered with stars whose colours were so intense and whose size so terrifying, that I toppled backwards and lost consciousness . . .

It is nothing, my dear Alexis, Laura told me, placing upon my forehead something cold that had the effect of an ice cube. Return to yourself and recognise your cousin, your Uncle Tungstenius and your friend Walter, who are urging you to shake off this lethargy.

No, no, it will be nothing, said my uncle, who was holding my wrist to take my pulse; but, another time, when you have talked a little too much at lunch while absent-mindedly drinking glass after glass of my little white wine from Neckar, do not amuse yourself by break-ing the glass display cases with your head and scattering all the crystals and gemstones of the collection like a mad-man. God knows what damage you could have done, if we had not been there, not to mention the fact that your wound could have been serious and cost you an eye or part of your nose! Mechanically, I raised my hand to my brow and when I took it away it was reddened with a few drops of blood.

Leave it alone, Laura told me, I am going to change the compress; drink a little of this kidney vetch, my child, and don't look at us in that wild, confused way. I am quite certain that you were not drunk, and that this is a little attack of apoplexy produced by an excess of unreward-ing toil.

O my dear Laura, I said with an effort, pressing my lips to her hand, how can you use the phrase 'unrewarding toil' to describe the admirable journey we made together into the crystal? Give me back that resplendent vision of the opal oceans and the lapis islands! Let us return to the verdant thickets of green chalcedony and the sublime banks of euclase and spinel, or to the fantastic stalagmites of the alabaster caves that invited us to such sweet repose! Why did you want to take me beyond the limits of the starry world and make me see things the human eye cannot bear?

Enough, enough! said my uncle sternly. This is fever, and I forbid you to say one word more. Go and fetch the doctor, Walter; and you, Laura, continue to cool his brain with compresses.

I believe I had a kind of sickness and many confused dreams, whose visions were not always pleasant. To be more precise, the assiduous presence of that good fellow Walter threw me into strange terrors. In vain, I tried to prove to him that I was not a madman, by giving him a faithful account of my journey into the crystal; he shook his head and shrugged his shoulders.

My poor Alexis, he said, it is a sad and truly humiliating thing for your friends and for yourself, that in the midst of healthy, rational teachings, you have become enamoured to the point of delirium with those miserable gemstones, good only for amusing children and amateur collectors. You are confusing everything in your mind, I can see that clearly, useful materials with minerals whose sole value is their rarity. You speak to me of fantastical colonnades of plaster and carpets of moss made from lead phosphate. There is no need to fall under the spell of hallucination in order to see these marvels at the heart of the earth, and the veins in the mines would offer your eyes, greedy for strange shapes and exquisite, brilliant colours, the treasures of antimony with its thousand azure needles, carbonated manganese in a rose eglantine crust, cerusite in pearly-white bundles, types of modified copper in every shade of the rainbow, from malachite greens to azurites of ultramarine blue; but all these coquetries of nature prove nothing, beyond chemical combinations which your uncle would call rational, while I call them fatal. You have not sufficiently grasped the goal of science, my dear child. You have stuffed your memory with vain details, and see, they have tired out your brain without any benefit to practical life. Forget your diamond peaks, diamond is just a little crystallised carbon. Coal is a hundred times more precious, and, by reason of its usefulness, I find it more beautiful than diamond. Remember what I told you, Alexis; the mattock, the anvil, the drill, the pick and the hammer, these are the most brilliant jewels and the most respectable forces of human reasoning!

I listened to Walter speaking, and my over-excited imagination followed him into the depths of the subterranean excavations. I saw the reflections of torches, suddenly illuminating veins of gold running along flanks of quartz the colour of rust; I heard the hoarse voices of the miners as they plunged into the galleries of iron or the chambers of copper, and their heavy steel sledgehammers' brutal rage as they beat mercilessly upon the most ingenious products of the mysterious work of centuries. Walter, who led this greedy, barbarous horde, looked to me like a Vandal chieftain, and fever ran through my veins, fear turned my limbs to ice; I felt the blows echo in my skull, and I hid my head in the pillows on my bed, crying out:

Mercy! Mercy! The mattock, the horrible mattock!

One day, my Uncle Tungstenius, seeing that I was calm, wanted to convince me also that my journey into the radiant regions of the crystal was nothing but a dream.

If you have seen all these pretty things, he told me with a smile, I congratulate you. That could be quite curious, especially the turquoise islands, if they derived from a gigantic accumulation of the remains of antediluvian animals; but you would do better to forget these fantastical exaggerations and study, if not more exactly, then at least more rationally, the history of life from its origin and throughout the entire course of its transformations on our globe. Your vision presented you only with a world that was dead or had yet to be born. You had perhaps thought too much of the moon, where nothing as yet indicates the presence of organic life. It would be better to think of that succession of magnificent births that are wrongly called the lost races, as if anything could be lost in the universe, and as if all new life was not a reworking of the elements of former life.

I listened more readily to my uncle than to my friend Walter, because, despite his stammer, he said some quite good things and did not have so much contempt for the combinations of shape and colour. Only, the sense of the beautiful, which had been revealed to me by Laura in our excursion through the crystal, was absolutely denied to him. He was open to enthusiastic admiration; but for him beauty was a state of being relative to the conditions of its existence. He fell down in ecstasy before the most hideous animals of the antediluvian ages. He was entirely at ease before the mastodon's teeth, and that monster's digestive faculties drew tears of affection from him. For him everything was mechanism, appropriation and function.

After a few weeks, I was cured and became fully aware of the delirium from which I had suffered. Seeing me become lucid again, people ceased tormenting me, and confined themselves to forbidding me to speak again, even in jest, about the amethyst geode and what I had seen from the summit of the great milky-white crystal.

In this regard Laura was unassailably discreet or stern. As soon as I opened my mouth to remind her of that magnificent excursion, she closed it with her hand; but she did not discourage me as the others did.

Later! later! she told me with a mysterious smile. Regain your strength, and we shall see if your dream was that of a poet or a madman.

I realised that I was expressing myself rather badly, and that this world that had seemed to me so beautiful was becoming ridiculous, viewed through the prosaic pedantry of my narration. I promised myself that I would train my mind and dull my senses to accept the language of the common man.

I had grown very attached to Laura during my illness. She had distracted me in my melancholy moments, reassured me in my nightmares, in a word, cared for me as if I had been her brother. In the state of weakness in which I had long foundered, the ardours of love had been able to seize hold of my imagination only in the form of fleeting dreams. My senses had remained dumb, my heart did not truly speak until the day my uncle announced my cousin's departure.

We were returning from the lecture, which I had attended for the first time since my illness.

You know, he told me, that we shall not be lunching

with Laura today. Cousin Lisbeth came to fetch her early this morning. She did not want anyone to wake you, thinking that you would perhaps feel a little sad at being separated from her.

My uncle believed naively that this little pang of regret would be aborted in the face of the fait accompli; he was most astonished to see me dissolve into tears.

Well, he said, I thought you were cured, and you are not, since you are affected like a child by such a small setback.

The setback was a stab of pain, I loved Laura. It was a true friendship, custom, trust, mutual understanding, and yet Laura did not embody the ideal woman my vision had left within me and which it would have been impossible for me to define. In the crystal I had seen her as taller, more beautiful, more intelligent, more mysterious than I now saw her again in reality. In reality, she was simple, good, cheerful, somewhat positive. It seemed to me that I could have spent my life perfectly happily by her side, but always hoping for a new impetus towards that enchanted world of the vision where she vainly denied having taken me. It seemed to me also that she was deceiving me to make me forget the too-vivid impression, and that the question of whether she would transport me there once more, when my strength permitted it, depended upon her affection for me.

Two years passed, during which I worked more fruitfully, but did not see Laura again. She had spent her holidays in the country, and, instead of joining her there, I had been forced to follow my uncle on a geological excursion to the Tyrol. At last Laura reappeared one summer's day, more beautiful and more amiable than ever.

Well, she said, holding out her two hands to me, you have not grown any more handsome, my fine Alexis; but you have the nice face of an honest boy, which makes you loved and respected. I know that you have become perfectly rational and that you are still hardworking. You don't break glass display cases with your head any more, on the pretext of walking through amethyst geodes and climbing escarpments of milky-white quartz. You see that, having heard you repeat them during your fever, I know the names of your favourite mountains. Now, you are becoming a mathematician, and that is more serious. I want to thank you and reward you with a confidence and a gift. You should know that I am getting married, and here is my wedding-gift, with my fiancé's permission.

As she said this, she pointed to Walter with one hand, while with the other she placed upon my finger the pretty white cornelian ring I had so long seen her wearing.

I stood there dumbstruck, and I have no idea of what I was able to say or do to express my humiliation, my jealousy or my despair. It is probable that everything concentrated itself within me to the point of making me appear decently disinterested; for, when I had suppressed the notion of what was surrounding me, I saw neither discontent, nor mockery, nor surprise on the well-meaning faces of my uncle, my cousin and her fiancé. I considered I had escaped lightly from a crisis that might have rendered me odious or ridiculous, and I went to lock myself away in my room with the ring, which I placed in front of me on my table, and which I contemplated with the bitter irony that circumstance demanded.

It was not a common cornelian, it was a very pretty hard stone, veined with opaque and translucent shades. As I looked at them questioningly, I sensed that they were extending around me, that they were filling my little room right up to the ceiling and that they were enveloping me like a cloud. At first I experienced a tiresome sensation like that of a fainting fit; but little by little the cloud lightened, spread out over a vast space and gently transported me onto the rounded top of a mountain, whose centre was all at once filled with a lively, red-gold blaze of light which enabled me to see Laura, seated beside me.

Friend, she said, talking to me in that language which she alone knew, and which had the gift of revealing itself to me suddenly, do not believe a word of what I said to you in front of our uncle. It is he who dreamed up this fable to prevent you from being distracted from your studies, seeing that we loved each other and that you were still too young to marry; but have no fear, I do not love Walter, and I shall never belong to anyone but you.

Ah! my dear Laura! I cried out, at last you have become radiant again with love and beauty, as I saw you in the amethyst! Yes, I believe, I know that you love me, and that

38

nothing can pull us apart. So why, in our family, do you always appear so incredulous or mocking?

I could also ask you, she replied, why in our family I see you as ugly, awkward, ridiculous, and poorly dressed, while in the crystal, you are as handsome as an angel and draped in the colours of the rainbow; but I do not ask you that, I know.

Teach it to me, Laura! You who know everything, give me the secret of appearing to you always and everywhere as you see me here.

My dear Alexis, it is with this as it is with all the secrets of the sciences you call natural: one who knows them can tell you that things are, and how they are; but when it is a question of why, everyone has his own opinion. I shall willingly tell you my opinion of the strange phenomenon which places us here together in broad daylight, while, in the world called the world of facts, we now see each other only through the shadows of relative life; but my opinion will be nothing but my opinion, and, if I told you it anywhere but here, you would regard me as a madwoman.

Tell it to me, Laura; it seems to me that here we are in the world of the real, and that elsewhere everything is illusion and lies.

Then, beautiful Laura spoke to me thus:

You must be aware that within each one of us who inhabit the earth there are two manifestations that are very distinct in reality, although they are confused in the notion of our terrestrial life. If consequently we believe that our senses are limited and our appreciation incomplete, we have only one soul, or, to speak like Walter, a certain animism destined to be extinguished with the functions of our organs. If, on the contrary, we raise ourselves above the sphere of the positive and the palpable, a mysterious, unnamed, invincible sense tells us that our self is not only in our organs, but that it is indissolubly linked to the life of the universe, and that it must survive intact beyond what we call death.

"What I remind you of here is not new: in all religious or metaphysical forms, men have believed and will always believe in the persistence of the self; but my idea, mine which I tell you about in the land of the ideal, is that this immortal self is contained only partially in the visible man. The visible man is merely the result of an emanation from the invisible man, and this, the true unit of his soul, the real, durable and divine face of his life, remains veiled to him.

"Where is it and what does it do, this flower of the eternal spirit, while the body's soul accomplishes its difficult, austere life of but a day? It is somewhere in time and space, since space and time are conditions of all life. In time, it preceded human life, and will survive after it, it accompanies and watches over it up to a certain point; but it is not dependent upon it and does not count its days and its hours within the same framework. In space, it certainly enjoys a feasible and frequent relationship with the human self; but it is not its slave, and its expansion floats in a sphere whose limits man does not know. Have you understood me?

I believe I have, I replied, and, to sum up your revelation in the simplest fashion, I shall say that we have two souls: one which lives within us and does not leave us, the other which lives outside us and which we do not know.

The first enables us to live in a fleeting way, and apparently dies with us, the second enables us to live eternally, and is unceasingly renewed with us. Or rather it is the soul which renews us, and which provides for the entire series of our successive existences, without ever becoming exhausted.

What the devil are you writing there? a harsh, discordant voice cried out beside me.

The cloud flew away, taking with it the radiant figure of Laura, and I found myself once again in my room, seated before my table, and writing the last lines which Walter was reading over my shoulder.

Since when, he added, have you been occupying yourself with philosophical nonsense? If you are claiming to make advances in practical science with this new genre of hypotheses, I cannot compliment you on it ... Now, leave that fine manuscript, and come and take your place at my engagement dinner.

Is it possible, my dear Walter, I replied, throwing myself into his arms, that, through friendship for me, you are taking part in a pretence unworthy of a serious man? I know perfectly well that Laura does not love you, and that you have never dreamed of being her husband.

"Laura told you she didn't love me?" he answered with a mocking tranquillity. That's quite possible and, as for me, if I am thinking of marrying her, I certainly haven't been doing so for long; but your uncle arranged it at a distance with his absent brother-in-law, and, as Laura did not say no, I had to consent to say yes ... Do not think that I am smitten with her; I don't have the time to put my imagination to work and discover fabulous perfections in that good little person. I do not dislike her, and, as she is extremely sensible, she asks no more of me for the moment. Later, when we have lived together for years, and we have allied our wills to run our household and bring up our children properly, I do not doubt that we shall have a good and solid friendship for each other. Until then, it is work to be placed in common with the idea of duty and the feeling of mutual respect. So you can tell me that Laura does not love me without surprising me and without wounding me. I would even be surprised if she did love me, since I have never thought to please her, and I would be a little anxious about her reason, if she saw in me an Amadis. Therefore, see things as they are, and be sure that they are as they must be.

I found Laura dressed up for dinner; she had a gown of pearl-white taffeta decorated with rose-pink gauze which reminded me confusedly of the soft, warm hue of the cornelian; but her face seemed to me demoralised, as though it were lifeless.

Come and give me confidence and courage, she said frankly, calling me to her side. I have wept a great deal today. It is not that I dislike Walter, nor that I am angry about marrying. I had known for a long time that I was destined for him, and I have never had any intention of becoming an old maid; but now the moment has come to leave my family and my home it is still painful. Be cheerful to help me forget all of this a little, or speak to me of reason so that I shall become cheerful, as I believe in the future.

How different Laura's language and physiognomy seemed to me from how they had been in the cloud emanating from the cornelian! She was so vulgarly resigned to her fate, that I clearly recognised the illusion of my dream; but, strange to tell, I no longer felt any pain at the thought of her really marrying Walter. I rediscovered the feeling of friendship that her care and her goodness had inspired in me, and I even rejoiced at the thought that I was going to live close by her, since she was leaving her home and coming to settle in our town.

The meal was very jolly. My uncle had placed it in the hands of Walter, who, as a positive man, knew how to eat well, and who had ordered it from one of the best cooks for hire in Fischausen. Laura had not been averse to busying herself with it too, and the governess had added to it with a few Italian dishes in her own style, strongly spiced and cooked in copious amounts of wine. Walter ate and drank enough for four. My uncle even became sufficiently jolly at dessert to perform a few courtly madrigals addressed to the governess, who was scarcely more than forty-five, and he wanted to open the dancing with her when Laura's young female friends demanded the violins.

I waltzed with my cousin. All at once it seemed to me that her face came alive with a singular beauty and that she was speaking to me with fire in the rapid whirlpool of the dance.

Let us leave here, she said to me, it's stifling; let us pass through those mirrors, which reflect back the candles' flame into the interminable distance. Don't you see that this is the image of the infinite, and that it is the road we must take? Come! a little courage, a leap forward, and we shall soon be in the crystal.

While Laura was speaking to me thus, I heard the mocking voice of Walter, who shouted out to me as I was passing close to him:

Hey! have a care! Not so close to the mirrors! Do you want to break those too? This boy is a veritable stag beetle, who beats his head against anything that shines.

Punch was being served. I was one of the last to approach, and found myself sitting next to Laura.

There, she said, handing me the chilled nectar in a fine goblet of Bohemian crystal, drink to my health, and look more cheerful. Do you realise you look as if you are bored, and that your distracted expression is preventing me from numbing myself as I would wish?

How can you want me to be jolly, my good Laura, when I see that you are not? You do not love Walter; why rush to marry without love, when love could come for him . . . or for another?

I am not permitted to love another, she replied, since it is he my father has chosen. You do not know all that has passed with regard to this marriage. You were considered too young to be informed of it; but, for myself who am even younger than you, you are not a child, and, since we were brought up together, I owe you the truth.

"We were originally destined for each other; but at first you proved too lazy, then extremely pedantic, and now, despite your goodwill and your intelligence, no one yet knows for what career you are best suited. I do not say this to cause you pain; I consider, myself, that no time has yet been lost with regard to your future. You learn, you have become hardworking and modest. You may well be a universal scholar like my uncle, or a specialised scholar like Walter; but my father, who wishes to see me married when he returns to settle near me, charged my uncle and my cousin Lisbeth with finding me a husband of an age suited to my own, that is a little older than you and engaged in very positive studies. He blames the unfortunate beginnings of his business career on ignorance and imagination, and he wants a son-in-law who is knowledgeable about some industry or other.

"Now my father, tired of voyages and adventures, seems satisfied with his position: he has sent me quite a nice sum of money for my dowry; but he did not wish to involve himself in setting me up. He claims he has become too much of a stranger to our customs, and that the choice made by my other relations will be better than one he could make himself or only advise upon.

"And so my poor mother's plans have been overturned, for she wanted to unite us; but she is no more, and one must admit that the present combination better assures my future and yours. You certainly do not wish to enter into married life so soon, and you have neither wealth nor a lucrative employment, since you do not yet even know what your vocation is."

You speak of all this with great ease, I replied. It is possible that I may rightly be considered a little young to marry; but that is a defect one can correct in oneself by willpower. If I had not been left in ignorance about all that you have revealed to me, I would have been neither lazy nor pedantic ... I would not have allowed myself to be dragged by Uncle Tungstenius into the examination of scientific hypotheses that his life and mine could not resolve, and into which moreover I was not perhaps borne by any special genius or enthusiastic passion. I would have listened to Walter's advice, I would have studied practical science and industrial craft: I would have made myself a blacksmith, miner, potter, geometrician or chemist; but not so many years have yet been lost. What my uncle teaches me is not useless: all the natural sciences are closely linked, and the knowledge of terrains leads me straight to the research and exploitation of useful minerals. Give me two or three years, Laura, and I shall have a position, you have my word upon it, I shall be a positive man. Can you not wait for me a while? Are you in such a hurry to marry? Have you no feelings of friendship for me?

You are forgetting one very simple thing, Laura went on: it is that, in three years' time, I shall also be three years older and that, consequently, there will never be the age distance between us that my father demands.

And, since Laura laughed as she said this, I lost my temper and reproached her.

You laugh, I said, and I suffer; but that is all the same to you, you love neither Walter nor me; you love only marriage, the idea of calling yourself "Madame" and wearing feathers in your hat. If you loved me, would you not make an effort to react against the will of a father who is probably not without feelings, and who is less wedded to his ideas than to your happiness? If you loved me, would you not have understood that I loved you too, and that your marriage to another would break my heart? You weep to leave your house in the country, and your cousin Lisbeth, and your governess Loredana, and perhaps also your garden, your cat and your canaries; but for me you have not one tear, and you ask me to be jolly so that you can forget your little customs among which my memory counts for absolutely nothing!

And, as I was saying this with scorn, turning my empty glass round in my clenched hand, for I dared not look at Laura for fear of seeing her angered against me, I saw all at once her face reflected in one of the facets of the Bohemian crystal. She was smiling, she was wondrously beautiful, and I heard her saying to me:

Calm yourself, you silly great child! Didn't I tell you that I love you? Don't you know that our earthly life is only a vain fantasmagoria, and that we are forever united in the transparent, radiant world of the ideal? Don't you see that Walter's earthly self is obscured by the acrid smoke from the coal, that this unfortunate has no memory, no presentiment of his eternal life, and that, while I enjoy myself on the serene heights where the prismatic light radiates the purest flames, he thinks only of burrowing into the dark shadows of stupid anthracite or into the muffled caverns where the frightful weight of galenite oppresses every seed of vitality, every flight towards the sun? No, no, in this life Walter will marry only the abyss, and I, daughter of the heavens, shall belong to the world of colour and shape; I must have palaces whose walls glitter and whose peaks shimmer in the free air and the full light of day. I sense incessant flight around me and I hear the harmonious beating of the wings of my true soul, forever borne towards the heavens; my human self could not accept the slavery of a union contrary to my true destiny.

Walter tore me away from the delights of this vision,

47

reproaching me for being drunk and gazing at my own image in the smoky crystal of my glass. Laura was no longer by my side. I do not know how many moments earlier she had left; but, until the moment when Walter came to speak to me, I had distinctly seen her charming image in the crystal. I tried to see Walter's there; with terror, I saw that it did not appear, and that this limpid substance was rejecting my friend's reflection as if his approach had changed it into a block of coal.

The evening was wearing on, and Laura had taken to dancing with a sort of frenzy, as if her lightness of character had wanted to protest against the revelations of her ideal being. I felt most fatigued by the noise of this little celebration, and I withdrew without anyone noticing. I was still staying in a part of the establishment separated from my uncle's lodgings by the botanical garden; but, as I had become assistant curator of the museum in place of Walter, who had been promoted, and as I exercised a jealous watchfulness over the scientific riches entrusted to my keeping, in order to reach my domicile I took the path which led past the mineralogical gallery.

I was walking along the glass cases, running the brightness of my candle over the pigeonholes, not looking in front of me, when I almost bumped into a strange person whose presence in this place, to which I alone had the keys, surprised me a great deal.

Who are you? I asked him, raising my lantern close to his face and speaking to him threateningly. What are you doing here, and how did you get in?

Calm this great anger, replied the bizarre stranger, and

know that since I belong to the house, I know its ins and outs.

You do not belong to this house, since I do, and I do not know you. You are going to follow me to my Uncle Tungstenius and explain yourself.

So, my little Alexis, went on the stranger, for it can only be you who are speaking to me, you take me for a thief! . . . Know that you are considerably mistaken, bearing in mind that the most beautiful specimens in this collection were furnished by myself, the majority of them given free of charge. Indeed, your Uncle Tungstenius knows me, and we shall go and see him shortly; but before doing so, I want to talk with you and ask for a little information.

I declare to you, I replied, that it shall not be so. You inspire no confidence at all in me despite the richness of your Persian costume, and I do not know the meaning of a disguise of this type on the body of a man who speaks my language without any trace of a foreign accent. You undoubtedly wish to lull my suspicions by pretending to know me, and you believe you will escape from me without my ensuring . . .

I believe, heaven protect me, that you are planning to arrest me and search me! replied the stranger, looking at me with disdain. A novice's fervour, my little friend! It is good form to take the duties of one's job to heart; but one must know whom one is dealing with.

As he said this, he seized me by the throat with an iron hand, not gripping me any tighter than was necessary to prevent me shouting and struggling; he made me leave the gallery, whose doors I found open, and took me into the garden without letting go of me.

There, he made me sit down on a bench and sat down at my side, telling me with a laugh that was as strange as his face, his clothes and his manners:

Well! do me the pleasure of recognising me and asking forgiveness from your Uncle Nasias for having taken him for a lock-picker. Recognise in me the former husband of your Aunt Gertrude and the father of Laura.

You! I cried out, you!

Nasias is my name abroad, he replied. I have just arrived from the depths of Asia, where—thanks to God—I did some rather good business and made some rather precious discoveries. Learn that I am now domiciled at the court of Persia, where the sovereign treats me with the greatest consideration because of certain rarities which I procured for him, and that, if I have broken off from my great occupations to come here, it is not with the intention of stealing from your little museum a few miserable gemstones with which the pettiest Indian rajah would not deign to decorate his slaves' toes or noses. Let us leave that, and tell me if my daughter is married.

She is not, I replied impetuously, and she will not yet be, if you consult her true inclination.

My Uncle Nasias took my lantern, which he had placed next to us on the bench, and raised it to my face as I had done to his a few moments earlier. His face was not precisely menacing as mine had been; it was rather mocking, but with an expression of icy irony, implacable, upsetting. As he took his time contemplating me, I also had the leisure to examine him in my anxiety.

In my childhood memories, Laura's father was a fat, blond, rosy-faced man, with a gentle, cheery face; the one my eyes now beheld was thin, olive-complexioned, of a type that was at once energetic and cunning. On his chin he wore a small, very black beard that looked rather like a goat's, and his eyes had acquired a satanic expression. He wore a tall hat of fine, jet-black fur and a robe of gold brocade, embroidered with incomparable richness. A magnificent Indian cashmere encircled his waist, and a yataghan covered with gemstones glittered at his side. I do not know if the Eastern sun, the great exhaustion of his journeys, the habitual great dangers and the necessity of a life mingled with cunning and audacity had transformed him to this extent, or if my memories were completely inaccurate: it was impossible for me to recognise him, and I was still in some doubt as to whether I was dealing with a bold impostor.

This suspicion gave me the strength to bear his keen gaze with a pride that suddenly seemed to satisfy him. He replaced the lantern on the bench and said to me calmly:

I see that you are an honest boy and that you have never sought to seduce my daughter. I see also that you are naive, sentimental, and that, if you love her, it is not at all from ambition; but, from what you say, you are in love and you would very much like to see me break the marriage to which I have consented for her. Embed this in your mind, my dear nephew, that, if I did break it, it would not be to your benefit, for you are only a child, and I do not find in your face any special energy which promises a brilliant destiny. So answer me disinterestedly, as you have nothing better to do, and with sincerity, since chance has caused you to be born an honest man: what of this other fellow Walter, of whom my brother-in-law

Tungstenius and his cousin Lisbeth wrote to me in such glowing terms?

Walter, I replied without hesitation, is the most worthy boy in the world. He is frank, loyal and his conduct is irreproachable. He has intelligence, learning and the ambition to distinguish himself in practical science.

And has he a profession?

He will have one in six months' time.

Very good, replied my Uncle Nasias, he is the son-in-law who suits me; but he will have the goodness to wait until he actually has the title of his employment. I am not a man to change my mind, and I am going immediately to tell him so and make his acquaintance. As for you, make haste to forget Laura, and, if you wish in a short space of time to become bold, intelligent, rich and active, prepare yourself to follow me. I am leaving again in a few days, and it is entirely up to you whether I take you along with me. Now let us go and see if the family will recognise me and give me a better welcome than yours.

I did not feel brave enough to follow him. I was shattered by fatigue. I was far from liking my Uncle Nasias and he seemed not at all favourable towards my hopes; but Laura's marriage had been delayed, and it seemed to me that in six months, immense events could surface and change the look of things.

When I awoke, with the first glimmers of dawn, I was surprised to see Nasias in my room, stretched out in my old leather armchair, and so profoundly asleep that I had the leisure to attend to my toilet before he had opened his eyes. He was so motionless and starkly white in the half-light of morning that, if I had seen him like that for the first time, he would have terrified me like a ghost. I approached him and touched him. He was singularly cold, but he was breathing very regularly and in such a peaceful manner, that his disturbing face was entirely changed. Like this, he seemed like the calmest of dead men and his strange ugliness had given way to a strange beauty.

I was preparing to leave soundlessly in order to go and attend to my duties, when he awoke of his own accord and looked at me without hostility or disdain.

You are surprised, he said, to see me in your bedroom; but you should know that, for more than ten years, I have not lain in a bed. That way of sleeping would be unbearable to me. It is as much as I can do if, from time to time, on my days of laziness, I sleep in a silk hammock. Moreover, accustomed as I am to a female companion, I do not like sleeping alone. Yesterday evening I found the door to your room standing ajar, and, instead of going to suffocate in the eiderdown Laura had had prepared for me at the height of summer, I came in with you, and took possession of this leather armchair which suits me very well. You snore a little loudly, but I imagined I was sleeping amid the roaring of lions roaming around my encampment, and you reminded me of nights of rather agreeable emotions.

I am happy, Uncle, I replied, that my armchair and my snoring agree with you, and please make use of them as often as you like.

I want to pay you back for your politeness, he went on; now come into my room, I have to speak with you.

When we were ensconced in the apartment which

Uncle Tungstenius had had made ready and which was the finest in the establishment, he showed me his luggage, whose smallness surprised me. It consisted entirely of a change of robe and hat, with a little case of underclothing made from yellow cloth, and an even smaller bronze box.

This, he said, is the way to travel freely from one end of our planet to the other, and, when you have adopted my habits, you will see that they are excellent. You must begin by becoming thin and losing the garish roses of your Germanic complexion, and for that, there is no better regime than eating little, sleeping fully dressed on the first chair you find, and never halting for more than three days under the same roof; but, before I take charge of your fate, which is no mean favour to do you, I want a few sincere explanations, and you are going to answer me as if you were standing before . . .

Before whom, my dear uncle?

Before the devil, ready to break your bones if you should lie, he replied, and his wicked smile and infernal gaze returned.

I am not in the habit of lying, I told him; I am an honest man, and I do not swear oaths.

Very well; then answer! What is the meaning of this story of a broken glass case, hallucinations, a journey into the crystal? During your illness two years ago, my brother-in-law wrote me something rather muddled about it and I made Laura tell me about it yesterday evening. Is it true that you wanted to enter by thought into a geode lined with amethyst crystals, that you believed you really had entered it, and that you saw there the face of my daughter?

All that is unfortunately true, I replied. I had an extraordinary vision, I broke a glass case, I injured my head, I had a fever, I recounted my dream with the conviction with which it had left me, and for some time people thought me mad. However, my uncle, I am not; I am cured, I am in good health, I work to my teachers' satisfaction, my behaviour is not at all extravagant, and nothing would have made me unworthy of being Laura's husband, if you had not given authorisation for her to be engaged to another who has little interest in her hand, whereas I . . .

This is not about Laura, said Uncle Nasias with a gesture of impatience; it is about what you saw in the crystal. I want to know what it was.

You want to humiliate me, I can see that clearly, make me say that I am not in possession of my wits, in order then to prove to me by my own admissions that I cannot marry Laura.

Laura again? Nasias cried out in anger. You bore me with your nonsense! I am speaking to you of serious things, you must answer me. What did you see within the crystal?

Since you take it thus, I told him, annoyed in my turn, what I saw in the crystal is more beautiful than what you have seen and will ever see in the course of your journeys. Here you are, proud and imperious as anything, because you have perhaps visited Oceania or crossed the Himalayas. Children's games, my dear uncle! Playthings from Nuremberg in comparison with the sublime, mysterious world that I saw as I see you, and which I explored, I who am talking to you!

Well done, that is how you must speak! went on my

uncle, whose angry face had once more become smooth and caressing. Now, tell on, my dear Alexis; I am listening to you.

Surprised by the interest he was taking in my adventure, and at the risk of being ensnared in a trap by him, I yielded to the pleasure of recounting what had left in me a memory so dear and so precise, a memory that no-one yet had deigned to listen to seriously. I must say that I had, this time, an incomparable listener. His eyes shone like two black diamonds, his half-open mouth seemed to drink in each of my words avidly; he leapt with enthusiasm, interrupted me with shouts of joy which were like roars, twisted like a grass snake with outbursts of convulsive laughter, and, when I had finished, he made me begin again and name each stage of my journey, each aspect of the fantastical land, asking me the relative distance, the extent, the height, the orientation of each mountain and of each valley, as if I were talking about a real country, one it was possible to explore other than on the wings of imagination.

When he had finished shouting out and I thought I could talk reason to him:

My dear uncle, I went on, permit me to say that you look to me like a man of great passion. That this land exists somewhere in the universe, I cannot doubt since I saw it and I can describe it; but that it may be useful to seek it on our planet, that is what I cannot believe. So we should not seek the path to it anywhere but in the divinatory faculties of our minds and in the hope of dwelling there one day, if our souls are as pure as diamond, the emblem of the soul's incorruptible nature.

My dear child, replied Uncle Nasias, you do not know what you are saying. You have had a revelation, and you do not understand it. You did not tell yourself that our little globe was a large geode, whose outer layer is our earthly bark and whose interior is lined with admirable, gigantic crystallisations, or had regard to those little protrusions on the surface that we call mountains, and which form no more than relative projections which the bumps on an orange skin present in relation to the size of a pumpkin. It is the world we call subterranean that is the true world of splendour; now, there certainly exists a vast part of the surface which is still unknown to man, where some tear or deep declivity would permit him to descend to the region of gemstones and to gaze in the open air upon the marvels which you saw in a dream. That, my dear nephew, is the sole dream of my own life, the sole goal of my long and difficult voyages. I am convinced that this tear or rather this volcanic crevasse of which I speak exists at the poles, that it is regular and in the form of a crater a few hundred leagues in diameter and a few dozen leagues deep, in short that the brightness from the mass of gems appearing at the bottom of this basin is the sole cause of the aurora borealis, as your dream clearly demonstrated to you.

What you are saying, my dear uncle, is founded on no healthy geological notion. My dream presented me on a large scale with known forms, forms that the mineralogical specimens placed before my eyes in miniature. Hence the kind of logic which led me into the enchanted world of the crystallo-geodic system. But what do we know about the interior conformation of our planet? We are as certain as we can be of only one thing: that is, that at thirty or thirty-three kilometres' depth, the heat is so intense that minerals can only exist in a fusible state. Supposing that one could descend to that depth, how would it therefore be possible for a man to avoid being burned to a crisp on the way, a state which, you will agree, is not favourable to the exercise of one's faculties of observation? As for the aurora borealis . . .

You are a schoolboy who wants to play the free thinker, my uncle went on. I forgive you that, it is how you are taught, and I know moreover that the famous Tungstenius claims to explain everything without taking account of the mysterious instincts that are more powerful in certain men than those deceptive faculties of observation about which your uncle is so vain. Separate yourself here and now from my brother-in-law's arid dissertations, and listen only to me, if you wish to raise yourself above a vulgar pedantry. You are a natural seer, do not torture your mind in order to render it blind.

"Know that I too am a seer, and that, before the sublime brightness of my imagination, I care very little for your little scientific hypotheses. Hypotheses, analogies, inductions, a fine business! I can make thousands of hypotheses for you, and all of them good, although they all contradict each other.

"Let us see! What is the meaning of your intense heat and your mineralogical materials in fusion at a depth of thirty-three kilometres? You proceed from known to unknown, and you believe that by so doing you grasp the key to all the mysteries. You know that at a depth of forty metres the temperature is eleven degrees, and that it rises by one degree centigrade per thirty-three metres. You make a calculation, and you reason on what happens at two or three thousand metres lower, without thinking that this heat you have detected is perhaps due only to the scarcity of air at the bottom of a well, while, in the great interior dislocations which are unknown to you, masses of air may circulate, considerable hurricanes which, for thousands of centuries, have fed certain volcanic fires, when at other points they had, with the aid of the waters, forever extinguished the energy of the alleged central fire. You know, moreover, that this central heat is not at all necessary to the earth's existence, since all life on the surface is the exclusive work of the sun. So, your core in a state of fusion is a pure hypothesis which hinders me little and which, moreover, I can counter, in supposing that there is an opening near the poles. If the poles are necessarily flattened because of the centripetal force which acts upon them continuously, why would they not be more deeply hollowed out than we think by the reaction of centrifugal force, which always operates in the direction of the equator? And if the poles are hollow down to a depth of thirty-three kilometres, which is in reality a trifle, how could the heat have existed there ever since the bottom of this abyss has been in contact with the icy climate of the region it occupies?

Permit me, Uncle; you speak of the icy climate at the poles. You must be aware that we believe today in the existence of an open sea at the North Pole. Travellers who have been able to approach it have seen floating mists and birds flying, certain indications of a mass of water free from the ice, and consequently enjoying a bearable temperature. Therefore, if there is appreciable depth, there is necessarily a sea, and if there is a sea or only a lake, there is no crater into which one might descend, and your hypothesis, for it is one far more random than all those of science, falls into the water, so to speak.

But, you imbecile, Uncle Nasias replied with brutal anger, every maritime basin is a crater, I do not say volcanic, but a crater, a cup of igneous origin, and, if you believe in the existence of a polar sea, you will grant me the necessity of an immense excavation to contain it. It remains to be seen if this excavation is empty or filled with water. Personally, I say it is empty, because any room for expansion will empty it continuously, and because it gives rise to the electrical phenomenon of the aurora borealis, a phenomenon about which I know you wished to speak to me. I agree that it gives off a gentle warmth, for, if you are absolutely wedded to it, I will allow you a burning core situated at the centre, and far distant from the geodic crystallisation which I intend to reach. Yes, I intend to, and I want to! I have travelled the equatorial world long enough to be very certain that the surface of the earth is extremely poor in gemstones, even in these relatively rich countries, and I am resolved to go and explore those where centripetal force holds in their boundless deposits and concentrates them, while centrifugal force only pushes back towards the equator miserable debris torn from the impoverished flanks of the planet, like those fragments of shattered bone which a man's swollen wounds throw out.

I confess that my Uncle Nasias appeared completely mad to me, and that I dared not contradict him, fearing he would fly into some act of rage.

Then explain to me, I said, to change the course of the conversation a little, what overpowering interest and burning curiosity impel you to search for these gemstone deposits which I won't qualify as imaginary, but which you will permit me to believe are difficult to reach.

You ask! he cried out vehemently. Ah! that is because you do not know either my will, or my intelligence, or my ambition; you do not know what patient and obstinate speculations enabled me to become wealthy enough to undertake immense things. I am going to tell you. You know that I left, fifteen years ago, as salesman for a firm that was trading in cheap jewellery with the naive peoples of the Orient. Our elegant mounts in pinchbeck and the shimmering cut of our little pieces of glass charmed the eyes of the half-savage women and warriors, who brought me in exchange antique jewels of incontestable value and real, fine stones of great price.

Allow me to tell you, my dear uncle, that this trade . . .

Business is business, my uncle went on without giving me the time to express my thoughts, and the fine people I was dealing with firmly believed for their part that they had taken me for a dupe. In certain localities where gemstones are found they thought that, in giving me a pebble they had picked up at their feet, they were mocking me, much more than I was really mocking them by giving them, in exchange for a gemstone that cost them nothing, a product of our European industry which, after all, had some value. They were even astonished by my liberality and, when I saw that they were on the point of becoming suspicious, I played at being mad, superstitious or at being a poltroon; but I pass over these details swiftly. All you need to know is that, from the little people, I passed quite quickly to the little sovereigns, and that my crystals mounted in copper turned their heads too.

"From success to success and exchange to exchange, I came to possess gemstones of great value and to be able to deal with the rich people of civilised countries. So I gave my trading house a good account of my mission; I assured them of useful relations with the barbarian peoples I had visited, and without ceasing to be useful to them, I created on my own account another industry which was to sell or barter real precious stones. In this trade, I became an expert lapidary and a skilful trader in curios; I made my fortune.

"I could henceforth take my ease, have a palace at Ispahan or Golconda, a villa at the foot of Vesuvius, or a feudal castle on the Rhine, and squander my income in a princely fashion without worrying about the North or South Pole, and without bothering about what is happening in your brain; but I am not a man for rest and a carefree life: the proof is that when I learned of your vision, I resolved to leave everything, risking the Shah of Persia's disfavour, to come here and question you.

And also to attend to your daughter's wedding!

My daughter's wedding is a detail. I have never seen my daughter in the crystal, and I have seen you there.

Me? You have seen me there? So you can see into it too?

A fine question! if not, would I believe in your vision? Crystal, you see, and by crystal I mean any mineralogical substance well and duly crystallised, is not what the common person thinks; it is a mysterious mirror which, at a given moment, received the imprint and reflected the

62

image of a great spectacle. This spectacle was that of the vitrification of our planet. Call it crystallisation if you will, it is all the same to me. Crystallisation is, according to you, the action by which the molecules making up a mineral unite after having been dissolved in a fluid? Whether this fluid be burning hot or frozen matters little to me, and I declare that with regard to primitive substances you know no more than I. I concede the igneous nature of the primitive world; but, if I grant you the existence of a still-active fire, I declare that it burns at the centre of a diamond, which is the core of the planet.

"Now, between this colossal gemstone and the granite crust which serve it as a gangue, galleries, grottos, immense gaps open out. This is the action of a withdrawal that undoubtedly left large empty spaces, and when calm was re-established, these empty spaces filled up with the most admirable and precious gemstones. It is there that ruby, sapphire, beryl, and all those rich crystallisations of silica combined with aluminium, in other words of sand with clay, soar up in gigantic pillars or hang from the vaulted roofs in formidable needles. It is there that the smallest stone outstrips the size of the Egyptian pyramids, and he who sees this sight will be the most fortunate of lapidaries and the most famous of naturalists. Now then, I saw this crystalline world in an escaped fragment of the treasure, in a marvellous gem that showed me your image at the same time as my own, just as you saw Laura's and your own in another gem. This is a revelation of an extra-scientific nature which is not given to everyone, and from which I intend to benefit.

"It is evident for me that we both possess a certain

divinatory sense which comes to us from God or the devil, it matters little, and which drives us irresistibly to the discovery and the conquest of the subterranean world. Your dream, more complete and lucid than mine, admirably specifies what I sensed: that is, that the gateway to the enchanted underground is at the poles and, as the North Pole is the less inaccessible, it is there that we must head as quickly as possible . . .

Allow me to catch my breath, my dear uncle, I cried out, my patience and politeness exhausted. Either you are mocking me, or you are mixing a few very incomplete scientific notions with the puerile chimeras of a sick mind.

Nasias did not explode as I was expecting. His conviction was so complete, that this time he was content to laugh at my incredulity.

We must put an end to this, he said, I must state a fact. Either you see in the crystal, or you do not see; either your sense of the ideal survives despite the stupidities of your materialist education, or these stupidities have extinguished it in you through your own fault. If the latter is the case, I shall abandon you to your miserable destiny. So prepare yourself to undergo a decisive test.

Uncle, I replied firmly, there is no need for a test. I do not see, I have never seen in the crystal. I dreamed that I saw my fantasies depicted there. It was a sickness I had, and which I no longer have, I feel, ever since you have sought to demonstrate the evidence of these futile phantoms. I thank you for the lecture you were kind enough to give me, and I swear to you that I will derive benefit from it. Permit me to go and work, and never resume a conversation that would become too painful for me.

You shall not escape my investigation, cried out Nasias, watching with amusement as I tried to open his door, from which he had previously—without my noticing—removed the key. I will not be fobbed off with defeats, and I have not come all the way from deepest Persia to depart again without knowing anything. Do not try to resist my examination, it is quite futile.

Then what is it that you demand, and what secret do you claim you will tear from me?

I demand one very simple thing: that you look at the object contained in this little box.

He then took a small key, which he wore upon his person, and opened the little bronze chest I had already noticed, and he placed before me a diamond of such prodigious whiteness, purity and size that it was impossible for me to bear the glare from it. It seemed to me that the rising sun was entering the room through the window and had just concentrated itself in that brilliant gemstone with all the power of its morning radiance. I closed my eyes, but to no avail. A red flame filled my pupils, a sensation of unbearable heat penetrated to the inside of my skull. I fell down as though struck by lightning, and I do not know if I lost consciousness, or if I saw in the reflection of that fiery gem something which I was capable of recounting . . .

There is a large gap in my memory at this point. It is impossible for me to explain the influence Nasias exercised over me from that point on. You must believe that I made no further objection to his strange Utopia, and his fantastical geological glimpses doubtless appeared to me like truths of a higher order with which I was no longer permitted to argue. Determined to follow him to the ends of the earth, I obtained only from him that he would make my Uncle Tungstenius promise not to dispose of Laura's hand before our return and, on my side, I swore not to confide in anyone, either at the moment of farewell, or by subsequent letters, the goal of the gigantic journey we were about to undertake.

That, at least I presume, is what passed between my Uncle Nasias and myself; for, I repeat, everything is confused for me in the journey that elapsed between the scene I have just recounted and our departure. I think I remember spending that day lying on my bed, annihilated by fatigue, and that, the next morning at daybreak, Nasias woke me, placed some kind of invisible amulet on my forehead, immediately giving me back my strength, after which we left the town without telling anyone and without taking the family's hopes and blessings with us, in short that we swiftly reached the port of Kiel. There, a ship belonging to my uncle awaited us, fully equipped for a long voyage across the polar seas.

III

I SHALL SAY NOTHING of our Atlantic crossing. I have every reason to believe it was happy and swift; but nothing could distract my absorbed attention, concentrated so to speak in a single thought: that of pleasing Nasias and meriting the hand of his daughter.

As for the world of crystals, I thought about it little of my own accord. My mind, paralysed at the seat of reasoning, did not attempt the least objection to the certainties my uncle set out before me with a singular energy and an ever-growing enthusiasm. His ardent suppositions entertained me like fairy tales, to the point where I could not always distinguish the results of his imagination from something real that might already have happened around me; however, our conversations on this subject always brought me to a singular state of intellectual and physical fatigue, and I found myself on the bed in my cabin, emerging from a profound sleep whose length I could not determine and whose fleeting dreams I could not retrace. I might have suspected my uncle of mixing some mysterious drug into my drink, submitting my will and my reason to his power in the most absolute way; but I had not even the energy to be suspicious. The mood of trust and infantile credulity in which I found myself had its own inexpressible charm, and I did not wish to resist it. Moreover I was, like the rest of the crew and its leader, full of health, well-being, courage and hope.

That is all I can say about myself up to the moment when my memories become clearer, and that moment arrived when our brig passed through the Northern Pillars of Hercules, situated, as everyone knows, at the entrance to the Smith Strait, between Cape Isabel and Cape Alexander.

Despite the frequency and intensity of the storms in that region and at that time of year, no serious danger had delayed our progress, nor compromised the strength of our excellent ship. Only, at the sight of the austere banks which rose up on either side of the channel, laden with mountains of ice more broken up and more menacing than all those to whose presence we had already grown accustomed, my heart skipped a beat, and the faces of the boldest sailors took on an expression of sombre reflection, as if we had entered the kingdom of death.

Nasias alone displayed an astonishing gaiety. He rubbed his hands, smiled at the terrifying icebergs as though they were old friends for whom he had been waiting a long time, and, if the gravity of his role as commander of the expedition had permitted it, he would have danced on the deck, despite the vigorous swell which constantly threw us about.

What can I say? he cried out when he saw that I was far from sharing his intoxication; are you already feeling the cold, and must I advise you on how to warm yourself up?

His face had suddenly become so despotic and so mocking, that I was terrified by this offer whose meaning I did not understand and which I did not wish to have explained to me. I shook off my torpor and put on a brave face until Cape Jackson, where we arrived not without fatigue, but without obstacles, in mid-August. Here, beyond the eightieth degree of latitude, Nasias decreed that we would over-winter in Wright Bay, towards the extreme north of Greenland. Very little time remained for us to prepare this harsh and perilous encampment. The days were shortening rapidly, and I do not know how, at this fluctuating edge of the navigable seas, we had been able to arrive so late without our way being blocked; as it was, we were touching the line of fixed ice, and scarcely had we entered the bay when we were seized as though by the immobility of the tomb.

Our crew, composed of thirty men, did not utter a single murmur. Apart from the fact that they regarded Nasias with an almost superstitious faith, the *Tantalus* (that was the name of the ship) was so well provisioned, so rich, so comfortable and so spacious, that no-one was afraid of spending a night there lasting several months. We settled in swiftly and in an orderly fashion, and on the day when the pale September sun appeared to us for an instant and then sank behind the faintly empurpled needles of the glacier called Humboldt, not to rise again for a long time, its funeral was celebrated on board with a veritable orgy. Nasias, who up till then had been so stern about discipline and so wisely economical with our resources, allowed the crew to drink until they were intoxicated, and to fill the muffled atmosphere of the darkness, and the mists that were closing in on us, with a savage din, songs and mad shouts.

Then he took me into his cabin, which was always perfectly heated, I know not how, and spoke to me thus:

You are no doubt astonished, my dear Alexis, by my imprudent behaviour; but you should know that everything is planned and that my actions are in no way random. This miserable crew, whose vociferous cries are shattering our eardrums, are destined to perish here, for from today they become perfectly useless to me and rather inconvenient. I intend to continue on alone with you and a band of Eskimo hunters, who are to join us this very night. Together, we shall continue my journey over the sea of pack ice to the open sea that is the sole goal of my labours. So prepare yourself to leave in a few hours and arm yourself with everything necessary to write down the details of our journey, which from now on will become interesting.

I remained stunned for a few moments.

Is that what you are planning, Uncle? I said at last, forcing myself not to sound indignant and so irritate the man to whom I had so imprudently entrusted my fate; are you not pleased to have reached unhindered a limit that no other ship before yours has been able to choose for its winter quarters, not to have yet lost a single man, nor seen any part of your provisions spoiled? How can you believe it possible to go further, during the sun's long absence, through the bitterest cold that wild animals can bear? How can you be so sure that you will see natives arrive, when you know that those unfortunates are now huddled several hundred leagues to the south, their igloos heated to ninety degrees? And, still more astonishingly, how can you countenance the idea of allowing such a valiant and excellent crew to perish here, scorning all the laws of God and man? This is one of those terrible jokes you have sworn to test me with, but which even a four-year-old child would not be taken in by; for, if you do not care about your brave travelling companions, you surely

70

do care a little, I imagine, about the means of returning to Europe and about a magnificent ship which cannot survive without daily maintenance and running repairs.

Nasias burst out laughing.

I see that your preoccupations are an agreeable blend of prudence and humanity. I see also that fear and cold have weakened your poor brain and that it is time to enliven you again by a method you are unaware of, but which has never failed to work upon you.

What are you planning to do? I cried out, terrified by his cruelly mocking gaze.

But, before I could reach the door of his cabin, he pulled from his breast the little bronze box that never left him, opened it, and promptly showed me the enormous diamond whose inexplicable effect had placed me in his power. This time, I bore its brilliance, and despite the unspeakable pain that the gem's heat produced in my head, I felt at the same time a kind of bitter sensual pleasure as I allowed it to enter me.

Very good, said Nasias, replacing it in the box, you are becoming accustomed to it, I can see that, and the effect is becoming excellent. Another two or three trials, and you will see into this pole star as clearly as into your poor amethyst geode. Now your doubts have been dispelled, your confidence has returned, and your touching sensitivity has been suitably dulled. Do you not also experience a certain pleasure in undergoing this sort of magnetic operation, which delivers you from the burden of your vain reason and the heavy baggage of your petty pedagogical science?

Now then, all goes well. I hear the delicious songs of

our new travelling companions. They will be here in a moment. Let us go and greet them.

I followed him on to the deserted deck, where a profound silence reigned, and, straining to hear, I distinguished in the distance the strangest and most horrible clamour. It was an immense yapping of sharp, plaintive, sinister, grotesque voices, and with each moment that passed the Sabbath was coming closer, as though borne by a gale. And yet the air was calm, and no breath of wind tore at the compacted mist. Soon, the invisible bacchanal was so close to us, that my heart skipped a beat with terror; it seemed to me that a band of famished wolves was about to lay siege to us. I questioned my uncle, who answered me calmly:

These are our guides, our friends and their draught animals, intelligent, robust and faithful creatures, which I did not want to squeeze on board, and which are coming to join us in accordance with the agreement made in southern Greenland.

I was going to ask my uncle at what stage of the voyage he had made this agreement, when I saw a multitude of red dots dancing on the ice around the ship's imprisoned flanks, and, by the muted glow of these resin torches, I was able to make out the strange companions who were reaching us. It was a band of hideous Eskimos accompanied by a band of dogs—thin, famished, hackles raised and more like fierce beasts than domesticated animals, harnessed in threes, fives or sevens to a long line of sledges of varying sizes, some of which were carrying light canoes. When they were within shouting distance, my uncle addressed the leader of the band in a loud voice:

Silence your beasts, put out your torches and line up here. Let me count you and let me see you.

We are ready to obey you, great chief *angekok*, replied the Eskimo, thus hailing my uncle with the title consecrated in his language to magicians and prophets; but, if we put out our torches, how will you be able to see us?

That does not concern you, replied my uncle; do what I tell you.

He was obeyed instantly, and that repugnant phantasmagoria of swarthy, stocky beings, misshapen in their sealskin clothes, those faces with their flattened noses, walrus mouths and fish eyes returned, to my great satisfaction, into the darkness.

All the same, the relief did not last long. A bright light, which for a moment I thought emanated from me, flooded the ship, the caravan and the ice as far as the eye could see, piercing or rather dispersing the fog around our encampment. I did not have to wait long to discover the cause of this phenomenon, for, as I turned back towards my uncle, I saw that he had placed upon his hat the magnificent eastern diamond which up to then had been so difficult to gaze upon, and now was as helpful to us as a portable star would have been; for, at the same time as it was lighting up the horrible night for a considerable distance, it was spreading a warmth as gentle as that of an Italian spring.

When they saw and felt this prodigy, all the Eskimos were stunned and delighted, and prostrated themselves upon the snow, while the dogs, ceasing the hoarse murmurs which had followed their piercing cries, began to yap and bound as a sign of joy.

You see, my uncle then said, you shall never lack for warmth or light with me. Stand up and send the strongest and least ugly among you up here. They shall load all the provisions your sleds can contain. I want only half the men; the rest will over-winter here, if that seems acceptable to them. I shall leave them this ship and all it contains when I have taken what I need.

Sublime *angekok*, cried out the chief, trembling with fear and greed, if we take your ship, will your crewmen not kill us?

My crewmen will not kill anyone, replied Nasias in a sinister voice. Come up without fear, but none of you must think of stealing the smallest item from what I intend to retain for myself, for at that same moment I shall set light to the ship and all those who are aboard.

And, to prove to them that he had the power, he tapped his diamond with his finger and made a jet of flame shoot forth from it. It flew into the air, sending out a rain of sparks.

I did not involve myself in the Eskimos' work, nor with loading their vehicles. In spite of the spell that enveloped me, I thought only of Nasias's mysterious words and the lugubrious silence that had long since succeeded the din of the orgy on the ship. There was not one sailor on deck. The man on watch and the helmsman had abandoned their posts. The natives' noisy arrival had not troubled any of our companions in their drunken slumber.

I understood clearly that my uncle was taking away or giving to the new arrivals all the food and all the clothes necessary to the crew. Was he also abandoning the lives of these now-defenceless unfortunates to them?

The Eskimos have no hint of ferocity in their character, but they are as voracious as sharks and as acquisitive as magpies. No doubt when they awoke our men would find themselves condemned to perish from cold and hunger.

My numbed conscience awoke. I resolved that if need be I would make the crew rise up in revolt, if it was possible to make them understand the situation, and rushed off into the refectory, where I found them all lying pell-mell on the couches or on the floor, in the midst of the debris of broken bottles and overturned tables.

What had happened at this sinister celebration? Blood, mixed with spilt wine and gin, had spread out to form an already glutinous lake about their motionless hands and their soiled clothing. It was an appalling scene of stupor or disaster succeeding some kind of frenzy of rage or despair. I called out in vain: around me reigned the silence of exhaustion . . . perhaps of death!

I touched the first face that presented itself to my hand; it was ice-cold. The smoking, blackened lamp poured an acrid smoke into this sepulchre, already filled with the stench of the orgy, and, askew on its base, dripped the last of its oil onto hair that stood on end in a final expression of horror. There was no other movement or sound; not a moan, not a death-rattle. They were all wounded, mutilated, unrecognisable, murdered by one another. Some had died while attempting a reconciliation, and lay with their arms entwined, after bidding each other a supreme and distressing farewell in wine-dregs and blood.

I was still standing there, petrified, before this horrible tableau, when I felt a hand take hold of me. It belonged to Nasias who led me outside, and as if he could read my thoughts:

It is too late, he said with a snigger; they will not rebel against the end that saves them from a slow death a hundred times more cruel than this one. I served them up the wine of rage, and, as they fought against imaginary enemies, they were able to console themselves with the dream of a valiant death. All is well with them now: the Eskimos will give them a tomb beneath the ice, as befits bold explorers. Now then, all is ready, follow me. Whether you like it or not, you can no longer go back.

I shall not follow you! I cried. You no longer have me under your spell. The crime you have just committed delivers me from your hateful ascendancy. You are a coward, a murderer, a poisoner, and, if I did not regard you as a madman . . .

What would you do to Laura's father? retorted my uncle. Would you then make her an orphan, and could you bring her back single-handedly from the depths of these desert wastes?

What do you mean? Is it possible that Laura . . .? No, no . . . You are insane!

Look! replied Nasias, who had led me on deck.

And I saw in an azure cloud the angelic figure of Laura standing on the top step of the companionway outside, preparing to leave the brig.

Laura, I cried, wait for me! Do not leave alone!

And I rushed towards her; but she placed a finger to her lips, and, showing me the sledges, she signalled to me to follow and disappeared before I was able to catch up with her.

Calm yourself, said my uncle, Laura will travel alone in a sledge which I brought along for her. It is she who henceforth will wear our pole star on her brow and who will lead our march to the north. We can only follow her at the distance it pleases her to place between her carriage and ours; but be sure that she will not abandon us, since she is our light and our life.

I followed my uncle mechanically, convinced that this time I was the plaything of a dream, and he made me get into the sledge reserved for me. I was alone in it, lying down in a sort of fur bed, and, although armed with a whip attached to my arm by a strap, I had no thoughts of using it. I was plunged into a strange torpor. I tried to turn over on my moving couch, as if to rid myself of an extravagant reverie: it was in vain; it seemed to me that I was bound hand and foot in my prison of fur. I tried to see the ghost of Laura again; all I could make out was a confused, far-off glow, and soon it became impossible for me to know if I was asleep or awake, if I had halted on the ice or on the earth, or had been borne away in a swift race by some unknown cause.

I do not know how much time I spent in that strange state. Since daylight did not appear and was not going to appear, and since mist hid the sky's aspect, I no doubt awoke and fell asleep again several times, without taking stock of the hours that passed. Finally I felt fully awake, and my vision cleared. The fog had completely disappeared, and the sky was sparkling with constellations whose position enabled me to determine the time with reasonable accuracy. It must be around noon, and I had come a long way, or else I had been travelling for several weeks.

I travelled over the ice, packed hard like a slab of marble, borne along by my dogs, which, without being directed, followed exactly in the tracks of two other sledges that had sped off at top speed. Behind me came the line of other sledges carrying the Eskimos and the supplies.

We followed a narrow ice-channel that ran between two fearsome ice floes, sometimes several hundred, sometimes several thousand feet high. A bright sapphire light seemed to emanate from these terrible environs; I saw them at last as they truly were, delivered as I was from all forms of fear and all moral appreciation of my situation. I felt neither cold nor heat, nor sadness nor terror. The air seemed gentle and smooth, my fur bed soft, and the light running steps of my dogs on the admirably level ground gave me a childish feeling of well-being.

As we passed we made no more sound in that lonely place than a flight of ghosts. I believe that the entire caravan slept deeply or abandoned itself like me to a nonchalant reverie. From time to time, a dog would bite its neighbour to prevent it slowing down, and that dog bit a third, as is the custom with these draught animals, a cry of canine anger would revive the ardour of a team, and called me back to the feeling of locomotion and of life; but these dry, swift sounds, deadened by the effect of the snow, were suddenly lost, and the absolute silence of the polar winter resumed its reassuring and solemn eloquence. Not a single cracking sound in the expanses of ice, not one dazzle of snow, nothing that might have given a warning of the horrible cataclysms which the thaw brings to these floating masses.

Was it the effect of an eternal twilight, or the magic of

these limpid blocks' reflections, or of some other phenomenon whose notion escaped me? I saw clearly, not as in the
full light of day, but as if by an electric light, sometimes
veiled in greenish-blue, sometimes enhanced with purple
or golden yellow. I could make out the smallest details of
the sublime setting we were crossing, and which, changing
in shape and aspect at each step, presented a succession of
marvellous tableaux. Sometimes the icebergs were cut up
into angular blocks, projecting immense canopies above
our heads, fringed with stalactites, sometimes their flanks
parted, and we passed through a forest of stocky, flaring
pillars, monstrous mushrooms surmounted by capitols
in a cyclopean style. Elsewhere, they formed slender columns, prodigious arches, regular obelisks, or were heaped
up on top of each other, as if they sought to scale the
heavens, then there were caves of a shimmering, ungrasp-
able depth, heavy pediments of native palaces guarded by
formless monsters. All the ideas of architecture were there
as though sketched out, then abandoned in an attack
of boundless delirium, or suddenly halted by hilarious
disasters.

These fantastic regions move the heart of man, because
he does not confront the implacable menaces without
having sacrificed his life, and because he feels shaken at
all times by forces which his science, his courage and his
industry have not yet been able to vanquish; but, in the
exceptional situation in which I found myself, my body
protected by an inexpressible well-being and my spirit
drowned in a still more astonishing feeling of security, I
saw only the grandiose, the curious, the intoxicating elements of the spectacle.

Little by little I grew accustomed to the charm of this vision of external things, and, returning to myself, I wondered if what my memory told me of recent events on my journey was indeed real. There was complete certainty in the present moment. I was indeed in a light bark sledge, lined with bear and seal skins, drawn by three dogs of admirable strength and ardour. There were indeed two other similar vehicles in front of me, one of which must contain my uncle Nasias, the other the caravan's guide, and the caravan was indeed behind us, following in our tracks. At the head of this caravan a light of inexplicable brightness was indeed travelling; but was this not some scientific lighting technique whose secret Nasias had not deigned to reveal to me?

My gaze fixed on the light radiating from the leading sledge, and I found nothing extraordinary in the fact that it carried a powerful lantern fed by seal oil, which the natives knew how to use to such good effect. Was it not insane to believe that a diamond could shine in the night like a lighthouse, and as for the agreeable warmth I was experiencing despite the climate, was that not probably due to a particular physical disposition? The horrible scene on the ship, moreover, was quite beyond belief. Up to that point my uncle, although stern, had shown his crew as much equity as solicitude. Our companions might indeed have got drunk to celebrate the start of their over-wintering, I might have seen them sleeping below decks; but the horror of their deaths, my uncle's insane and cruel words, his unbelievable agreements with the Eskimos, and, finally and most crucially, the sudden appearance of Laura on the *Tantalus*, deep in the polar seas, all this bore the stamp of the most complete hallucination.

The thought that I was subject to attacks of madness threw me into great sorrow; I resolved to observe myself carefully and to make the greatest efforts to preserve myself from them.

An event of the most positive kind finally gave me back my sense of reality. We were making a stop on an islet, in the shelter of a magnificent rocky cave; we had just emerged from the floe's frozen channel. My uncle got down from the sledge which was travelling in front of me; I hastened to look at the person who was emerging from the sledge in front of him, and, seeing the size and features of a frightful dwarf shaped like a truncated Hercules, I was unable to prevent myself laughing sadly at myself. I inwardly asked forgiveness from Laura for having seen her spectre in this grotesque Eskimo figure, and I waited for someone to come and untie me; for I was indeed truly bound hand and foot by sturdy thongs to my moving bed.

Well, my uncle said cheerily as our men were lighting the fire and preparing the meal, how do you feel now?

I have never felt better, I replied, and I believe I am going to eat most heartily.

Then that will be the first time in the two months since we left the ship, he replied, feeling my pulse; for, if I had not fed you with good broth in tablet form and piping hot tea, you would have died of hunger, so completely had the fever removed your sense of self-preservation. I was right to tie you on firmly and to attach your dogs' reins to my sledge, you would have been mislaid on the way like a parcel. At last you are well once more, and you will not speak to me again, I hope, of the abandoned ship, the crew destroyed by a frenetic poison, nor of my daughter hidden on board in a trunk and condemned to act as our guide towards the arctic pole.

I asked forgiveness from my uncle for the stupid things I must have said during the fever, and I thanked him for the care he had given me without my knowing.

We ate a copious meal, and I was no longer astonished to see our provisions so abundant and fresh when I learned that they had been renewed several times *en route* by fortunate encounters with animals caught unawares in the snow, and night-birds attracted by the bright light of our lantern. I learned also that we had been constantly favoured by the brilliant phenomena of the pole's electrical light, and, emerging from the cave, I was able to convince myself with my own eyes of the splendour of that natural form of lighting.

My uncle smiled at the chimeras I had harboured and the fact that I wished to confess to him in order to deliver myself from them once and for all.

Man is indeed a child, he told me. The study and examination of nature are not enough for him. His imagination must furnish him with puerile legends and fictions, while the miraculous rains down on him from the sky without any magician having anything to do with it.

At that moment, my Uncle Nasias seemed to me to be a perfectly right-minded, rational man.

While we were conversing, our men were building us a house. The roof of the cave was covered with a layer of ice thick enough to protect us from the winds getting in, they closed its entrance with a wall of snow-blocks, cut with remarkable speed and skill. Thus sheltered and well-warmed, we stretched out in our nice dry sledges, in the midst of our well-fed dogs, and rested as completely and as restoratively as marmots in their burrow.

I think back over that night of warmth, well-being and security in the polar ice fields as one of the most astonishing of my journey. I had the strangest dreams that night. I saw myself at my Uncle Tungstenius's home. He talked to me of botany and reproached me for not sufficiently studying the fossil flora of the coalmines.

Now that you are travelling through lands that have been so little explored, he told me, you may find plants that are as yet unknown, and it would be indeed curious to compare them with those whose carboniferous schists have preserved their imprint for us. Come now, leave that sledge that madly wrecks our garden paths for a while; tie up those aggressive dogs that lay waste our borders. Try to find the *oppositifolia saxifrage* in those polar lichens; you shall make a bouquet of it for your cousin Laura, who is to marry on Sunday.

I tried to show my Uncle Tungstenius again that I could not be simultaneously in the realm of the polar saxifrages and in our botanical garden at Fischausen, that my dogs, who were sleeping on an islet in the Kennedy Strait, were no threat at all to our borders, and that Laura could not marry in the absence of her father; but he appeared to be in a most bizarre state of mind and in no way encumbered by the problem of ubiquity.

Just then Walter came, and entered so completely into my Uncle Tungstenius's opinions on this matter, that I allowed myself to be convinced and consented to show them how the Eskimos beat the snow to make a sort of stone which withstands the intense heat of their dwellings, since this sort of artificial gemstone is the only kind of bed they have. In order to try it out at home, all we had to do was obtain some snow in high summer in our garden at Fischausen; for in my dream, time was also ubiquitous, and the June roses were in full bloom in the flowerbed.

We were engrossed in seeking this unlikely snow, when Laura brought us a great armful of eider feathers, assuring us that one could satisfactorily beat and solidify this material; to which we made no objection, and, when we had succeeded in turning it into a tablet fifteen feet square, the wind penetrated the opening of the cave which had crumbled away, and dispersed all the eider feathers to great peals of laughter from my cousin, who collected them in handfuls and threw the flakes in my face.

These imagined things provided entertainment, if one may call it such, in my slumbers; but I was woken by a joyful clamour. Our Eskimos, who were already up—for it would have been broad daylight, had we not been enveloped by the inflexible polar night—had spotted a group of wild geese that had just come down on our islet. These birds, tired or lacking discernment, allowed themselves to be caught by hand, and a veritable massacre was carried out: a pointless act of cruelty which revolted me, for we were not short of food, and the number of our victims far exceeded what we could eat and carry away with us. My uncle found my sensitivity misplaced, and mocked it so disdainfully that my suspicions returned. I saw flashes of ferocity pass across his usually grave, gentle physiognomy, reminding me of the scene, or the dream of the scene, on the ship. As for me, I was upset to see the destruction of these phalanxes of travelling birds whom my uncle classed as stupid and which were not wary of human stupidity, for they came to throw themselves into our hands as if to ask us for protection and friendship.

After a few days' rest and feasting in the cave, we set off again, still travelling northwards on ice that was polished and shining almost everywhere. The fever took hold of me again the moment I was in my sledge, and, sensing that my mind was wandering, I bound myself to my vehicle in order not to succumb to the desire to abandon it and venture into the lonely, savage wilderness. I do not know if we had re-entered the mist; if the polar light had been eclipsed or if our lantern had gone out.

We travelled as if at random in the darkness, and I felt frozen with terror. I could see nothing in front of me, nothing behind; I could not even make out my dogs, and the quiet sound made by the wake of my own sledge did not reach me. At times I imagined that I was dead and that my poor self, deprived of its organs, was being borne away to another world solely by the impetus of its mysterious potentiality.

We were still moving forward. The darkness receded, and the moon or some dazzling white star that I took for the moon came to show me that we had entered an ice-tunnel, a few leagues in length. From time to time, a fissure in the roof or a break in the wall allowed me to make out the immensity or the narrowness of this sub-glacial passage; then everything disappeared, and, for quite a long time, which sometimes seemed to me to last more than an hour, we plunged back into the most complete, terrifying darkness.

During one of those moments, I felt a sudden attack of lassitude, despair or irritation. Deciding that I would never see the light again and telling myself that I was blind or mad, I began to untie myself with the vague intention of delivering myself from existence; but all at once the icy roof ceased to shelter me, and I distinctly saw Laura travelling close to me. I scarcely had the strength to let out a cry of joy and to stretch out my arms to her.

Forward! forward! she shouted to me.

And mechanically I whipped my dogs, although they were already doing at least six miles per hour. Laura was still travelling on my right, outrunning me by at most one or two paces. I saw her face clearly, for she turned it constantly towards me to make sure that I was following her. She was standing up, her hair streaming out, her body enveloped in a cloak of grebe feathers which formed thick, satiny folds about her, like new-fallen snow. Was she on a sledge or carried by a cloud, pulled by fantastical animals or supported by a snow-flurry at ground level? I could not be sure; but for quite a long time I saw her, and my whole being was renewed. When her image vanished, I wondered if it had not been my own that I had seen reflected on the shining wall of ice along which I was travelling; but I did not want to give up a vague hope of seeing her again soon, however insane it might be.

The various encampments and monotonous events of our journey have left few traces in my memory. I can scarcely gauge its length, as I am not certain of the date when we left the ship. I know that one day the sun reappeared, and that the caravan halted, shouting out for joy.

We were on terra firma, at the summit of a high, mossy cliff; behind us, the immense glaciers of the two banks of the strait which we had crossed stretched out as far as the eye could see to the south, and before us, the open ocean, limitless, dark blue, broke at our feet, on harsh volcanic rocks, with a fearsome sound. Never had music by Mozart or Rossini been sweeter to my ears, so much had the dismal silence and solemn rigidity of the ice fields frustrated my need for external life. Our Eskimos, drunk with joy, erected the tents and prepared the equipment for fishing and hunting. Clouds of birds of all sizes filled the pink sky, and we saw innumerable whales frolicking in the warm tides of the polar sea.

Others had reported and consecrated it before us, this long-problematic sea; but, almost alone, at the end of their strength and in a hurry to retrace their steps, so as not to succumb to the fatigue and perils of the return journey, they had merely greeted and glimpsed it. We had arrived at this limit of the known world all in good health, rich in munitions, having lost none of our dogs, and with none of our precious equipment damaged. It was a such an unlikely conjunction of circumstances, that the Eskimos regarded my uncle more and more as a powerful magician, and that I myself, forced to admire his foresight, his skill and the faith that had sustained him, gazed upon him with a superstitious respect.

The sun paid us a short visit that day; but its appearance in a sky all marbled with shades of pink and orange had given me back my confidence and cheerfulness. For a long time the sea was lit up by a twilight that was transparent as amethyst; we looked for a place sheltered from the wind, and at the foot of a glacier of immaculate whiteness we chose a charming valley carpeted with a fresh, velvety moss in which flowered lychnis, hesperis, lilac saxifrages, dwarf willows and Bermuda blue-eyed grass.

The following day, having noted that the seawater was as warm as in temperate climes, we gave ourselves the pleasure of bathing. I then climbed up onto quite a high peak with my uncle, and we took greater stock of the unexplored land we wished to reach.

This land was the west bank of the strait we had crossed, which stretched out in a straight line to the north on our left, while on our right the northern lands of Greenland seemed to flee away in a concave, horizontal line. In front of us lay nothing but the limitless sea. The western coast, also low-lying over a long distance, rose up again in powerful volcanic masses, the Parry Mountains no doubt, already seen from far off and christened by those who came before us, but never reached.

We have done nothing, said my uncle, if we do not go that far; we have two good canoes, and indeed we shall go; how does that seem to you?

We shall go, I replied; even if, as I believe, we find only lava and ice, we shall certainly go!

If we did not find anything else there, went on my uncle, it would be because your divinatory sense and mine had been obliterated, and then we should have to go back to mankind's incomplete and tardy practical science to discover, in five or six thousand years perhaps, the secret of the polar world; but if you have doubts, I do not: I have consulted my diamond, this mirror of the globe's interior, this revealer of the invisible world, and I know what incalculable wealth awaits us, what glory lies in store for us, erasing all of humanity's past and present glories!

Uncle, I said, fascinated by his conviction, let me look at it too, this diamond whose bright light, which your eyes can penetrate, has been too powerful for my weak sight up to now. Make haste, the sun is already setting. Let me strive to raise myself to the heights of your vision.

Gladly, said my uncle, presenting me with the gemstone he called his pole star. From the moment when you at last believe and submit, you will be able to read this talisman as well as I can.

I looked at the diamond, which suddenly seemed to me to take on the proportions of a mountain in my hand, and I almost fell off the top of the cliff into the sea when I saw in it the image of Laura, perfectly clear and clad in her ideal beauty. Standing, dressed all in pink, smiling and animated, she executed a great triumphal, gracious gesture, showing me a far-off peak well beyond the Parry Mountains.

Speak! I cried out, tell me . . .

But the sun was disappearing into the purple of the sea's horizon, and I could no longer see anything in the diamond but the sky and the waves.

Well, what did you see? said my uncle, taking back his treasure.

I saw Laura, and I believe, I replied.

We resolved to wait until the days were longer. Our encampment was most agreeable and abundantly provided with game and firewood. The shore was covered with drift-wood debris, and the mountains were clad in a thick layer of lichen. I was extremely surprised to see the remains of powerful vegetation beached on this coast.

I, said Nasias, am surprised only by your surprise. Beyond these far-off banks whose details our eye questions in vain, I do not doubt that there exists an Eldorado, an enchanted land where the cedars of Lebanon are wedded to gigantic laburnums and perhaps to the richest products of tropical nature.

My uncle's assertion appeared a little risky to me, and I keenly regretted having neglected the study of botany, which would have enabled me better to analyse the plant remains I had before me. It seemed to me that I could sometimes recognise among them the stems of tree ferns, sometimes the overlapping bark of immense palm trees; but I was not sure of anything, and I lost myself in conjectures.

After the pleasantest of camps, we were disposed to undertake the crossing of the polar sea, when our Eski-mos, who up till then had been so confident and joyful, remarked to us that, given the time needed for the return journey and the exceptional warmth of the year, we ran the risk of being caught in the thaw, which would make the route impracticable by sea and by land.

My uncle showed them in vain that what they took for an exceptional summer was only the effect of a cli-mate that was new for them and stable in this region; that in case of a sudden thaw, we were in a position to wait for weeks and months for the propitious moment; they mutinied. Nostalgia had gripped them, they missed their desolate climes, their dens under the snow, their rancid, salted fish, perhaps also their relations and their friends. In short, they wanted to leave, and they did not return to obedience until they were faced with Nasias's threat. He presented them with his diamond, telling them that it would dry them all out and cook them, if they began complaining again. We had only two canoes. It was very difficult for us to get them to build others with the drift-wood and the bark from the shore. These enchanted trees terrified their imagination. And then they said that this navigable sea, rich in fish on the coasts, must, at a certain distance, contain unknown monsters and treacherous whirlpools.

Their true object of horror was basically the fear that we would bear them away into the world of Europeans, which they assumed was situated in the neighbourhood of Cape Bellot, never to see their homeland again. My uncle, despite his prestige and his authority, could only persuade a dozen of them to follow us. We managed to equip six canoes and, forced to abandon all our equipment and all our chances of returning to the discontented troop, we set out and abandoned ourselves to destiny.

Although the weather was magnificent, a strong swell prevailed on that sea, where no vessel had yet ventured and will perhaps never venture again. Our own strength and our rowers' was soon exhausted, and we had to abandon ourselves to a strong current which all at once carried us northwards with a terrifying swiftness.

We went round the Parry Mountains without being able to land, and, after three days of absolute desperation on the part of our men, who however lacked for nothing, did not suffer from the cold and took no blades on board their excellent canoes, at sun-up we saw a prodigiously high peak appear, which my uncle felt surpassed many of the summits in the Himalayas.

Our courage returned; but, when the night hid this giant of the world in its shadows, the fear of not being able to find it again and going past it in spite of ourselves was painful.

Only Nasias displayed no anxiety. Our canoes, tied together with ropes, were moving in convoy, but at the vagaries of chance, when the sky and the waters were filled with a light so bright that it was difficult to bear. It was the most magnificent aurora borealis our eyes had yet gazed upon, and for twelve hours its intensity did not weaken for a moment, although it presented infinitely varied phenomena of colour and shape, each more magical than the previous one. Only the famous crown, which is noticed in these palpitations of the polar moon, remained completely stable and entirely distinct, and we were able to convince ourselves that it emanated from the place where the peak was situated, for the peak had come back into sight and rose to a point in the very middle of the luminous circle, like a black needle in a gold ring.

Admiration and surprise had silenced fear. Impatient to reach this magical world, our Eskimos did their best to paddle, although the powerful current overtook their vain attempts. When daylight returned, they became discouraged again: the peak was as far off as the previous evening, and it even seemed to recede as we moved forward. We had to journey thus for several days and several nights; finally this terrifying summit seemed lower: this was a sure sign that we were getting closer. Little by little other, smaller mountains loomed up from the horizon. Behind them the principal peak was entirely masked, and a land of considerable extent was unfurled before our eyes. From that moment on, each hour we approached was an hour of growing certainty and joy. With the telescope, we made out forests, valleys, waterfalls, a land luxuriant with vegetation, and the heat became so real, that we had to take off our furs.

But how could we land there, in this promised land? When we were well within sight of it, we saw that it was surrounded by a vertical cliff two or three thousand metres high, plunging straight down into the tide, smooth as a rampart, black and shining like jade, and nowhere offering the slightest gap through which one might have hope of penetrating. Close up, it was much worse. What had seemed shiny to us in these black walls was indeed so, for this compact belt was made up of large crystals of tourmaline, some of which had attained the size of our largest towers; but, instead of in places presenting horizontal ledges where one might hope to find depressions arranged in natural steps, these bizarre rocks were planted like the quills of a porcupine, and their tips pointed towards the sea like the cannon-mouths of a fortress of giants.

These shining rocks, some black and opaque, others transparent and the colour of sea-water, were set into an impenetrable mountain, and very finely striated with delicate fluting. They offered a spectacle so strange and so rich, that I now thought of nothing but gazing at them, and yet we had already spent an entire day travelling along them, without being able to get through the furious waves which broke upon them, and without spotting the slightest sign of shelter on that impregnable coast.

Finally, towards evening, we entered for good or ill into a sort of channel, and we came to land at the narrow, rocky end of a small cove where our canoes were shattered like glass, and two of our men killed by the shock they received as they and their vessel beached on the ground.

This ominous landing was nonetheless hailed with shouts of joy, although the survivors were all wounded or bruised to some degree; but we were rendered almost insensible to the loss of our unfortunate companions by the terror of this prestigious voyage, the thirst which tortured us, our fresh water supplies having been exhausted thirty-six hours previously, the despair which had more or less gripped all of us, apart from just one, the indomitable Nasias, and finally by I know not what savage enthusiasm for the peril braved and vanquished.

Wet, broken, too tired to feel hunger, we threw ourselves onto the dark shore without asking ourselves if we were on a reef or on solid ground, and we spent more than an hour like this without speaking, without sleeping, without thinking of anything, occasionally laughing in a stupid manner, then falling back into a fearful silence beside the furious wave which covered us with sand and foam.

Nasias had disappeared, and I alone had noticed his absence; but suddenly the sea lit up with sparkling fires, and we saw the splendid boreal crown form at the zenith; we were inundated as if enveloped by its immense irradiation.

To your feet! shouted Nasias's voice above our heads. Here! here! Come, climb up, accommodation and feasting await you!

94

We were suddenly brought back to life, and we slowly climbed a short ravine, which brought us into a narrow valley filled with unknown trees and grasses. A myriad birds flew around Nasias, who had found their nests on a rocky ledge and filled his robe with eggs of all sizes. They ranged from ones the size of a roc's eggs to those the size of a goldcrest's. To this feast were added samples of magnificent fruits, and, showing us the trees and the bushes where he had gathered them:

Go, he said, make your own harvest too. You may confidently eat this flavoursome produce, which I have already tested upon myself; there are no poisons here.

So saying, he bent down, tore up a handful of dried grasses with which he stuffed his pipe, and calmly began to smoke, spreading around us exquisitely scented puffs of smoke, while we were stilling our hunger and thirst by eating the most delicate eggs and the most agreeable fruits.

It would have been easy for us to feast on meat, as the birds were just as lacking in timidity as those on the Kennedy islet; but no one thought of that at first, so great was our initial hunger. When it was satisfied our Eskimos, who had learned foresight by dint of dangers and terrors, wanted to wring the necks of these poor birds, which reproached us with eloquent cries for the theft of their eggs. This time, Nasias was energetically opposed to the murder.

My friends, he said, here one does not kill; you must take that as read. The earth produces in abundance all that is necessary to man, and man has no enemies here, unless he makes them.

I do not know if our companions understood this admonition, which I judged excellent; overcome by sleep, they fell asleep on the ground, which was made up of a fine dusting of talc. I followed suit, for I did not have the superhuman strength of Nasias, who left us and did not reappear until daylight came.

IV

WHEN HE AWOKE ME, I was very surprised not to find any of my companions around me.

I no longer had need of them, he told me calmly, I sent them away.

Sent them away? I cried out, stunned. But where to? How? By what means?

What does it matter to you? he replied with a snigger; surely you cannot be interested in those coarse, voracious and stupid individuals?

Yes indeed, as much as and more, to be sure, than in faithful and submissive domestic animals. Those ten men and the two we lost when we landed here were the elite of our troop; they showed great courage and patience. I was beginning to understand their language, to become accustomed to their costumes, and even those of them who scarcely had human faces harboured truly human feelings. Tell me, Uncle, where have you sent them? This land is doubtless an Eden where they can wander with nothing to fear.

This land, replied Nasias, is an Eden that I am in no way planning to share with beings that are unworthy of possessing it. Those brutes would not have lived here three days without bringing us into conflict with all the animal forces of nature. I have sent them away; accept that you will never see them again, nor their canoes, their companions, their sledges and their dogs. Here and over all the sea that encloses us we are absolute monarchs. It falls to us alone to find a way of leaving when it so pleases us. There is no hurry, we are quite comfortable here. Get up, take a bath in this charming stream, which murmurs two paces from you, gather your meal from the first branch you find, and let us think about exploring our island, for it is indeed an island set apart from any visible continent and hollowed out like a cup, as I told you; only, there is a prodigiously tall volcano in the middle; but it is a natural beacon of electric light and nothing more.

All objections, all recriminations, were perfectly useless. I was alone in this unknown world with a man who was stronger, more intelligent, more implacable and more of a believer than I was. I must not fight him, but equal him, if that were possible for me to do.

I cast a last glance behind me, and, climbing up onto a promontory, I looked again at the place where we had landed. Either the sea had turned them to dust, or Nasias had saved and hidden them, but there was no trace of our vessels. As for the men, what had become of them? Even the imprint of their footsteps in the sand had been wiped away. I looked down at my feet, and saw light pools of blood; my hands were impregnated with it. I shivered and asked myself if, like my unfortunate companions from the *Tantalus*, I had not taken part in some frightful scene of delirium and carnage.

Nasias, who was watching me, began to laugh, and, picking a wild blackberry the size of a pomegranate, he squeezed out the juice before me.

What you see there, he told me, are the traces of your supper last night.

I wanted to question him further; he turned his back

on me and refused to answer. I must indeed submit to him. As he had already explored the surrounding area, he had one goal, and he headed towards it. I followed him in silence, without weapons or munitions, and as if we had conquered a land where man has nothing left to conquer.

Nevertheless it was not long before we encountered beings that would have been infinitely formidable, had they shown any hostility towards us: these were bison, mouflon, reindeer, aurochs, and elands far larger than those known to us, and all belonging to species which had been entirely lost on the rest of the planet. There were even several that should not have been called by the names I have given them, unsure which one is appropriate for them, for almost all appeared to me to be intermediaries between types which had vanished and present-day fauna. We saw no reptiles there, nor carnivorous animals. As for these great herbivores, which moved in immense herds through the grassy or marshy regions, they were content to look at us with a touch of astonishment, but without fear or aversion. They scarcely bestirred themselves to let us pass, and we could have drawn them at our leisure, had we been armed with the necessary drawing equipment.

In any case, Nasias paid them scant attention and did not allow me to stop for very long. I followed him regretfully, for, now that we were in no danger of any kind, no one was waiting for us anywhere any more, and we belonged entirely to this new life into which we had resolutely thrown ourselves, I scarcely knew what we were looking for any more, and why my uncle, instead of being content with seeing his premonitions made real within the

limits of the possible, still insisted on pursuing their chi-
merical aspect. I shared my reflections with him at my
own risk and peril, for he had become imperious, feverish,
wild, and I saw clearly that in the event of open resistance,
he would not hesitate to rid himself of me. He scarcely
answered me, or, when he deigned to explain, it was to
reproach me bitterly for my lack of faith and the wilful
dulling of my most precious faculties.

What struck me most in the region we were crossing,
was not that we constantly encountered new species within
all types of animals, plants and minerals: that was to be
expected in these latitudes; it was seeing them grow in size
as we walked northwards and this fact, which destroyed all
my rational notions, could not be explained except by the
rapid increase in the heat of the climate. Nevertheless we
had not yet reached the region of humid heat and gigantic
development.

We had reached the high plateaux supported by the
tourmaline cliff. Once again the central peak appeared to
us in all its splendour; but it was impossible for us to make
out its base, which lay in a misty circle. I calculated that
it was five or six good days' walk away, assuming that we
could reach it in a straight line; and, assuming again that it
occupied the central part of the island, I calculated that in
this direction this island was at least one hundred leagues
in diameter.

After two days' march, during which we continued to
walk across hills that were easily climbed, we halted on
a last high point, from where the entire island was laid
out at our feet. It was a magnificent view of the place as
a whole. This entire land had resulted from an immense

movement of the earth, which took place in various different geological periods. I was able to make out the traces of great volcanic disturbances; but, in general, the primitive stages were laid bare, and the sedimentary lands occupied only a small surface area. Moreover, none had resisted violent dislocations or the continuous action of a general subsidence, increasingly marked by crumbling the more the eye inspected the central point, which now presented only a terrifying collection of confused ruins.

After three or four days we left the fertile regions inhabited by quadrupeds. The shady ravines and forests picturesquely spread over imposing rocks, the narrow ravines irrigated by lively waters and dotted with bright flowers, were succeeded by interminable slopes of peaty meadow so deeply waterlogged that the herbivores no longer ventured there, and it soon became impossible for us to go any further.

As these slopes—which were probably supported by a wall of tourmaline equivalent to that which extended on the other, maritime, side—overhung the bottom of the cirque, we could only assume there were considerable freshwater courses running along the lower part of our plateaux. The parts ahead of us seemed more arid; but the distance was too great for us to be certain.

Forced to halt and sustain ourselves with purslane and mosses, which moreover were extremely good, we were thinking about retracing our steps to seek an easier slope, when I was terrified by a roaring sound of such a peculiar nature that no comparison with the cries of animals we know can describe it. It was like the prolonged sound from a belfry, mixed with the purring of a steam-powered machine. As I was looking around on all sides, I heard this sound above my head and saw something so enormous fly over, that instinctively I ducked down so as not to be struck by this incomprehensible being as it passed by.

It came down close to us, and I recognised an individual that—apart from its unfeasible size—appeared to me to belong more or less to the genus *megalosoma*. It was the size of a buffalo, and it had, moreover, a buffalo's flat horns and dark pelt. Although this monster caused me real terror, I could not prevent myself admiring it, for it was in all respects a fine animal. Its wing cases and its impenetrable cuirass were clad in a thick olive-green fur highlighted with gold, and from its back rose up that majestic, fork-shaped framework made of horn that is characteristic of the male. Only it appeared not to notice our presence, and began to browse around us as a tame animal might do; then it raised its powerful wing cases, opened up the folds of its broad, iridescent, gauzy wings, and, without rising more than two or three metres, set off and landed a few hundred feet further away.

That animal, which nothing astonished, must live on foliage, said Nasias, for it did not enjoy browsing on the low plants that grow here, and it disdained them. I would have thought that, having left the forested areas we have just crossed ourselves, it was going to go back up there, but it is descending towards the arid deserts. So the nooks and crannies of this great heap of shattered rocks must conceal leaf-bearing plants, and consequently a healthy soil. I regret now not having climbed on to the back of that *coleoptera*, whose heavy but steady flight would have spared us much futile walking.

That is a fantasy we can manage without, I replied, showing my uncle a dozen of those same scarab beetles, which were flying above us and seemed to be following the one which had served as their scout.

We must reach the place where they will land before they fly off again, for, if they do the same as the first one, they will not make long flights.

Indeed the scarab beetles landed quite close to us, and we were able to approach without alarming them. I do not know if our images appeared quite clear to them, through the horny substance that covered their eyes. They seemed very stupid to us, and, although they could have crushed us with their terrible mandibles or torn us apart with the sharp hooks of their claws, they allowed us to mount without resisting. We chose two good-sized males, seated ourselves on the corselet, our arms and legs in the forked horns to hold us on securely, and allowed ourselves to be carried off without a trace of emotion. This mode of riding is very gentle; only, the sound of the wing casings and the wind produced by the wings are disagreeable in the extreme.

I think, I said to my uncle the first time we set foot on the ground, that the future colonists of this island will use the *megalosoma* only to carry burdens. It seems docile enough to obey an instruction and even . . .

What are you saying about colonists? cried my uncle with a shrug of his shoulders. Do you by chance imagine that I have spent so much, and confronted so many dangers, to bring a few days' wealth to this stupid human species, which knows only how to lay waste and sterilise the richest of nature's shrines? We would not have more than a handful of men here for a month before they blindly wiped out these rare and curious animal species and destroyed the beautiful essences of the forests, instead of husbanding them. Man is an animal that does more evil than all the others, do you not know that? No, no! let us leave the beasts in peace, and keep for ourselves alone the discovery of this precious island.

And yet, I went on, I do not see that we, who are only two, are absolutely respecting these animals' freedom. I do not know if they like carrying us, and you must agree that, in your thoughts, they seem most appropriate to help you transport the riches you intend to discover.

Not in the least, replied Nasias. The riches I wish to discover will stay where they are until I have taken the measures necessary for me to appropriate them. This entire island, with all it contains in its flanks, belongs to me; no-one will exploit it but my slaves, and, if I need many of them, I shall find many.

In any other circumstances, I would have combated my uncle's antisocial and anti-human theories; but my *megalosoma* was heavily raising its wing-casings and beginning to make them purr. I hastily climbed astride and took the beast by the horns, never was an expression more literally exact, and several consecutive flights brought us to the edge of the tourmaline ravine, as I had anticipated. There, our large *coleoptera* were of great help, for without them we would never have been able to descend that wall, bristling with gigantic crystals.

Scarcely had we reached the bottom of it, I admit not

without a touch of vertigo on my account, when we saw a broad, raging torrent, gushing through magnificent forests; but, instead of taking us across it, the *megalosomae* landed on some trees resembling monkey-puzzles, five hundred metres tall, and began greedily sucking their sticky bark. Their fantastic progress through the sharp-bladed leaves of these giant plants rendered our situation impossible, and we had to leave our mounts and—cautiously and slowly—climb down from branch to branch until we reached the ground.

There, we found flowers and fruits completely different from those of the higher regions. Instead of the berries of rosaceous plants, which had formed the basis of our diet in previous days, we found types of edible thistle with flesh resembling the artichoke and the pineapple, and the eggs of birds (we did not see a single one in these forests) were replaced by butterfly larvae of extraordinary size and a most refined taste.

But we had to get across the river, and we were fortunate in spotting on its banks some amphibious tortoises between five and six metres long. These allowed us to climb onto their carapaces, and, after several rather annoying spontaneous halts on the islets that were dotted all over the river, they brought us slowly to the other bank.

Those are basically good creatures, although lazy, said my uncle, seeing them head back into the water. They are worth more than men; they do not refuse work and they ask nothing for their trouble. The more I think about it, the more I tell myself that men will serve my exploitation but I shall not allow my brutish slaves to inconvenience the animals.

We took an entire day to cross this forested region, which was admirable in its power and majesty. There, we saw only evergreen trees, hollies, conifers and diverse species of gigantic junipers. Frightful reptiles crawled in the mass of dried needles that hid the ground from us; but these animals appeared harmless to us, and we crossed the woods without having to engage in any battles.

The further we advanced, the more resolution and confidence Nasias showed, while I felt some unknown, secret horror seizing hold of me. In its male beauty, this unexplored world had an increasingly menacing physiognomy. In vain the animals proved indifferent to the sight of and contact with man. This very indifference had something so scornful about it that in my mind the feeling of our smallness and isolation increased tenfold. The dome formed by some trees, beside which the most beautiful cedars of Lebanon would have looked stunted; the thickness of the plant-stems; the length of the reptiles which crossed the clearings and which shone in the cold shadows like streams of greenish silver; the rough shapes and oversized thorns of the low-growing plants; the absence of birds and quadrupeds; silent flights of insanely large bombyx and geometer moths; the humid and debilitating atmosphere; the murky daylight which seemed to fall regretfully upon a heavy carpet of hundred-year-old debris; great ponds of standing water where monstrous frogs stared at us with glassy, stupid eyes; all this seemed to say to us: "What are you doing here, where man is nothing and where nothing was made for him?"

At last, in the evening, we found ourselves in an open area, and by the light of the boreal crown, which was becoming more and more intense, we saw that a large lake separated us from the base of the peak. This destroyed all the fantasies my uncle had cherished about the existence of an accessible opening, and confirmed the opinion I had formed for myself when I saw the cone emerging from a circle of mist.

For the first time, I saw that Nasias was discouraged, and, as he remained silent, I was emboldened to speak to him directly. Why had he not foreseen that a deep cavity, wherever in the world it might be, might not serve at all as a reservoir for watercourses, rain or melting snow? I even allowed myself a few jokes which I felt the need to express; for my association with this strange man was merely a series of revolts against my reason, at each moment paralysed by the vertiginous ascendancy which had control over me.

He was wounded to the quick, and I think for a moment he was minded to put an end to my doubts, for he was as irritated and as tired with them as I was with his irresistible authority; but he calmed down after spewing out a torrent of coarse insults, which I had in no way expected from such a reserved man.

Now, he said, we are both wrong this time; that is why I forgive you. I faltered for a moment, and was punished by a fit of anger that risks diminishing my intellectual and physical powers. Man's worth resides only in his faith. Take back yours or you are lost.

And he gave me the diamond to look at. Immediately the image of the cone surrounded by purplish flames appeared there as if I was touching it, and, in that iridescent lake surrounding the base of the peak, I made out indefinable but perfectly solid ground, on which Laura was walking confidently and inviting me to follow her. This vision produced its accustomed effect upon me: it transported me into the delicious realm of the impossible, or rather it dispelled like a deceptive cloud that word impossible, written at the threshold of all discoveries.

Let us leave now! I said to my uncle. Why stop here? Does night reign in these privileged parts? Our powers are increased tenfold by the effect of the electricity which radiates from everywhere here. Do they have need of six hours' rest? Let us keep on walking, let us walk forever. I know where we are going now. Laura awaits us on the opal lake. Let us make haste to join her.

We walked all night, which was moreover very short, for I estimate that we were at eighty-nine degrees latitude and that we were approaching the days when the sun is above the horizon for six months.

At sunrise, a terrifying and sublime sight greeted our eyes. There were neither mists nor rocks heaped up at the base of the peak, and we could make out perfectly the circular shape of the gulf out of which it soared up to the clouds. This gulf was indeed filled by a lake; but one splendid detail we had not been able to fix upon was a circular waterfall, equally well supplied around its entire rim. It emerged from a cave, also circular, then hurtled down into the lake from a height of twelve to fifteen hundred metres. This marvel of nature threw me into ecstasy, but singularly annoyed Nasias.

Certainly, he said, it is a very beautiful thing and without its like in the known world; but I could gladly have done without it. We have arrived too late. Some unforeseen cataclysm has opened the waters' path to the gaping mouth of the terrestrial axis.

Did you flatter yourself then, I said wryly, that you would find an underground passage, a practicable tunnel from one pole to the other? No doubt you have seen such a thing in those cardboard globes pierced by an iron skewer, and you perhaps dreamed that our earthly globe revolved on a strong bar magnetised at both ends. I dreamed of that also when I was six years old; but you will permit me to doubt it today and to find it entirely natural that a vast region of peaty mountains arranged in a cirque should have its circular outflow in the deepest place. If yesterday we crossed a healthy, fertile terrace, that was because it was saved from perpetual flooding by the river we crossed on tortoise-back, and because that river plunges down somewhere beneath an eminently compacted soil, and then swirls in invisible caverns below our feet.

What a marvellous explanation! said Nasias contemptuously, throwing me fierce looks. So, either you did not see into the diamond properly, or you lied to me. You did not see Laura walking on those deceptive waters, you have never seen anything with common sense and you have mocked me. Misfortune to you, ignorant schoolboy, rebellious and inconvenient companion, misfortune will fall upon you, I swear it, if it is so!

Wait, I told him firmly; do not be in a hurry to eliminate me and send me to join the crew of the *Tantalus* and our Eskimo canoeists. There may be a way of settling things and reconciling all our hypotheses. Do you have a sensitive ear? Do you believe that at the distance we are from that colossal Niagara you would be able to hear its roar?

Yes, most certainly! cried out my uncle, throwing himself into my arms, I would hear the powerful din of those gushing waters, and I hear nothing at all! That waterfall is frozen.

Or petrified, my dear uncle!

You have, he went on, a stupid way of joking, but at heart you see fairly clearly. That circular torrent may be a terrible effusion of cold lava, and we must find out for sure; forward!

We then entered the region of sterile debris. It was, on a large scale, a flood of porous lavas and tephrines, like those broad currents one finds in the Auvergne and which occupy so much surface area between Volvic and Pontgibault, according to my Uncle Tungstenius. I remember his description, which had appeared grandiose to me, but which seemed very mean before the expanse of volcanic nodules that rose up before me as far as the eye could see, and which simulated the appearance of boiling fluid suddenly petrified at the peak of its activity. It was like a sea whose waves had changed into stony mounds or innumerable standing stones. This entire ocean of bare rocks had a uniform colour, desolate, livid, and one would have taken the short, greyish lichen whose leprosy marbled it, for the remains of a rain of cinders that the wind had forgotten to sweep away. That day was difficult, nothing to eat or drink. I know not how our strength did not desert us.

At last we reached the limits of this kingdom of death, where what we had taken at a distance for a belt of cacti or gigantic reeds was merely an efflorescence of enormous pumice stones, calcified into the most bizarre shapes. The lake stretched out beneath our feet, the waterfall gushed from all directions around us, and its vast waves were no more than an admirable, milky-white vitrification, with hints of translucent opal. But how were we to descend it? Our jagged path around it jutted over every side; it was fearfully high, and we were exhausted by fatigue, hunger and thirst. In a fold of the ground, I noticed a trail of debris and soon a small area where plants grew, including the creeping roots of a kind of pink milk vetch. These roots were an unhoped-for gift to us from Providence. After eating some, and noticing how long and tenacious they were, I sought some out and found some which had grown to several metres in length. I made an ample harvest, and my uncle, delighted with my idea, helped me to make them into a knotted rope, fifty yards in length. When we tried it out, using a block of lava tied to the end, we saw that it was quite strong, but too short by half to reach one of the first ledges of the glass waterfall. We had to spend the night where we were, in order to devote the entire next day to lengthening our ladder. My uncle seemed resigned to this, and I prepared myself a bed of asbestos in a conveniently cup-shaped hollow in the rocks. Nasias treated me like a sybarite.

I am, I replied, because I consider that we are arriving at our greatest peril. I am not too bad a walker on an empty stomach, as you have seen; but today I have little strength in my arms, and, despite my childhood escapades, I consider myself a very bad acrobat at this moment. However, nothing can shake my resolution to descend into that abyss. So I need all the vigour I am capable of, and, moreover, if I am to be shipwrecked in port and if I am to sleep my last night here, I should like to savour it and spend it well. I would advise you, my dear uncle, to do likewise.

Scarcely had I lain down, I dare not say gone to sleep, for I had never felt more awake, Walter came and sat down beside me without my experiencing the least surprise at seeing him there.

Your undertaking is insane, he told me; you will break your bones and will find nothing interesting in this bizarre place. This is without doubt a remarkable example of the power of volcanic ejections; but all the mineral materials of this recently-cooled fire have undergone such a degree of cooking, if one may use such a term, that it will be impossible for you to define their nature. Moreover, how will you bring back specimens that we can submit to analysis, when you are so far off knowing how you will bring yourself back?

You speak well, I replied; but, since you were able to come and find me here, you have some means of transport that you will no doubt consent to share with me.

I did not have much difficulty in climbing the staircase to your room, Walter went on with a smile, and, if you were to make an effort of reason, you would recognise that only your spirit is at the arctic pole, while your body is seated at your table and your hand is writing mad words which I am amusing myself by answering.

You mock me, Walter, I cried out, or else it is your spirit that casts itself madly back to our home and our customs in Fischausen: do you not see the polar crown, the great peak of obsidian and the white, milky sea which surrounds it?

I see only the shade of your lamp, he replied, and your pyramid-shaped inkwell with its faience bowl. Come, rouse yourself to the sound of Laura's piano; at this moment she is singing a ballad to her father, who is quietly smoking his pipe at the drawing-room window.

I rose to my feet impetuously. Walter had disappeared, the opal sea was shining at my feet, and the aurora borealis drew an immense rainbow above me. Nasias, who was seated some distance away, was in reality smoking his pipe, and I could distinctly hear Laura's voice and the notes of her piano. This mixture of dreaming and waking tormented me for part of the night. Laura's voice, so sweet in my memory, at that moment took on a shocking reality, for Laura could scarcely sing, and she had a little childish lisp which rendered serious music comical. Only in the crystal were her words free from this defect. Impatient, I stood at the window of my bedroom and shouted to her across the garden not to murder the *Ballad from Saul*. She paid no heed, and in a pique I lay back down on my bed of asbestos, where, blocking up my ears, I finally managed to fall asleep.

When I awoke, in broad daylight, I saw that Nasias had worked unstintingly and that our root-rope had reached the required length. I helped him to attach it securely, and wanted to be the first to test it. I descended without hindrance, helping myself with my feet when I could make contact with a projection in the lava. In this way I reached a little platform, which the rope did not reach far enough past to render it unnecessary to pull it down and reattach it once more. Bending over the edge, I saw below me a heap of ashes, white as snow, and I did not hesitate to let myself fall into it. This ash was so crumbly, that I disappeared into it completely; but shaking myself, I emerged safe and sound, and shouted to my uncle to follow suit.

He descended with the same success, and we hastened to cut off a good-sized length of rope to take away and eat when we needed to, for it would take us eight or ten hours to cross this lake of glass, and as you can imagine, we saw no trace of vegetation.

Soon the sun heated up this gleaming surface so much, that the glare became unbearable to our eyes, and the heat atrocious to our feet; but we could not retrace our steps: we were halfway through the journey, and we continued to walk with a stoicism of which I would never have thought myself capable. The reflection from the circular waterfall was so burning-bright, that it seemed to us that we were at the centre of the sun. Fortunately, a gust of wind dislodged an avalanche of snow from the summit of the central peak, sending it rolling down towards us. We set our course to reach it before walking became impossible, and this unhoped-for help enabled us to arrive almost at the base of the cone.

There a prodigious surprise awaited us, or rather a bitter disappointment. For a long time, it had seemed to us that we were walking on the puffed-up volcanic crust, with the hollow sound of emptiness underneath. We saw then that this crust, suddenly interrupted, was an enormous distance from the peak and the subsoil, that we were walking on an increasingly thin vault, and that it was impossible to go forward without it breaking beneath our feet like an earthenware plate. In his impatience, Nasias broke it five or six times and almost fell in. I managed to calm him down and talk to him. It was quite pointless to reach the cone, for it did not serve as an entrance to any cave, and it did not seem ever to have served as the mouth to a volcano.

On examining it at closer quarters, which we had not been able to do before, we saw that this formidable peak, crowned by a glacier with keen needles, was none other than a rectangular prism of pale green, dazzlingly bright olivine, but homogeneous and of one block from the base to the summit.

We ate some of the rope, and I made my uncle promise to take a few hours' rest. As soon as the night had cooled our lake of opaline glass a little, we would cross it again, we would go and fetch our root-rope, we would come back before the heat, if possible, and we would decide whether to descend to the bottom of the invisible abyss beneath our feet. This reasonable proposition did not suit the fervent Nasias at all.

If I am to perish here, he replied, I want to see what lies between us and that accursed peak.

And leaping onto the fragile glass, he began to shatter it with furious kicks, picking up the largest fragments he could lift and throwing them with all his strength so as to break up a larger surface area.

Seeing that we were lost, I now thought only of hastening the moment of our destruction. I joined forces with my uncle in his wild enterprise and, shattering the last, undulating sections of the glass lake, I managed to detach a considerable mass, which tumbled down into the abyss with the sound of windows breaking and at last enabled us to see the bottom.

What a strange and grandiose sight greeted our eyes! Beneath the vitreous layer stretched an ocean of colossal stalagmites: violet, pink, blue, green, white and transparent as amethyst, as ruby, sapphire, beryl and diamond. The great polar cavern my uncle had dreamed of was in fact a geode, lined with glittering crystals, and this geode extended for an immeasurable distance beneath the earth's crust!

This is nothing! he said with perfect coolness. We are seeing only a small corner of the treasure, one edge of the earth's colossal inner world. I aim to descend into it and possess all that it hides from men's obtuse minds, all that it conceals from their vain and timid greed!

What will you do with it? I said with the same coolness, for we had arrived at that paroxysm of intellectual exaltation, which in him produced the triumphal calm of sated ambition, and in me the most complete philosophical disinterest. I do not know if the treasures we are glimpsing have a real value among men; but I assume that these are indeed mines of crystals the size of Egyptian obelisks, as you predicted: what use will they be to us in this deserted land, which we shall certainly never be able to leave?

We came here, therefore we shall be able to go back, said Nasias with a laugh; what is worrying you? Does the island lack wood to make new canoes?

But neither you nor I know how to make a canoe, and still less how to use one. So do you know where we shall find our Eskimos? Tell me, what have you done with those poor fellows?

The same as I did with the crew of the *Tantalus* and the same as I am going to do with you! cried Nasias, suddenly seized with convulsive laughter.

And, lapsing into utter madness, he leapt towards the edge of the great cavern, let out a great shout, and disappeared into the abyss, taking with him thin, sonorous shards from the lake of glass.

For a few seconds I heard crackling sounds. Then the noise made by Nasias and the crystals as they fell faded to nothing. I called to him, I could not believe what my own senses were telling me. My voice was lost in the desert's horrible magnificence. I was alone in the world!

I stood there, petrified. It seemed to me that my feet were rooted to the spot, that my limbs were stiffening, and that I was turning into crystal myself.

What are you doing here? Laura asked me, laying her hand on my brow. Are you sleepwalking? How could you believe that man Nasias's lies? He has never been my father. He is a madman, fulfilling his destiny. God grant that he is gone forever, for his malign influence paralysed mine, and since you have been with him, I have rarely been able to make you see and understand me. Come, let us go, and have no more fears about food or shelter; with me, you shall no longer know those vulgar impediments to life and the mind: do I not have a dowry? Are you curious to enter this little geode we call the Earth? It is quite pointless, it is such a small thing! But if it amuses you, I shall happily lead you there, since it is an artist's curiosity, a poet's fantasy, and not base cupidity that drives you. I know the way to these subterranean splendours, and there is no need to break one's neck in order to see them at close hand.

No, Laura, I cried, it was not a poet's fantasy or an artist's curiosity that brought me here. It was your voice that called me, your gaze which led me, it was the love that I have for you . . .

I know, she said, you wanted to win my hand by obeying that man Nasias who is nothing but a miserable impostor and the worst kind of sorcerer, while my true father will certainly consent to grant it to you when he knows that I love you. You have travelled many roads and braved many dangers, my poor Alexis, to seek the happiness that awaited you at home. Do you wish us to return there immediately?

Yes, immediately, I cried.

Without seeing the inside of the geode? Without traversing the world of colossal gems, lit by the eternal radiance of its electrical light? Without climbing to the top of that obsidian or hornblende cone, taller than the Himalayas? Without verifying for yourself that the weather is tropical at the North Pole, and that the heart of the globe is agreeably cool? And yet it would be most curious to find out all these things, and most glorious to be able to state them before our Uncle Tungstenius and all the learned men of Europe!

Although it seemed that Laura was making fun of me, I did not want her words proved false.

I believe in the existence of all these marvels, I replied; but, though I am on the very point of seeing them for myself, I shall renounce doing so, if you so wish, and if by that sacrifice I can obtain your father's consent to my happiness one hour sooner.

That is good, said Laura, holding out her two charming

hands to me. I can see that in the midst of your madness, you love me more than anything in the world, and that I must forgive you everything. Come.

She approached the gulf which had swallowed up Nasias, and telling me to "take the ramp", she began to walk down into it as if a staircase had formed beneath her feet. I followed her as though down a ramp, which was no doubt imaginary, but which saved me from vertigo, and in this way we entered the Earth's interior.

At the end of about an hour, Laura, who had forbidden me to speak to her, made me sit down on the last step.

Get your breath back, she said, you are tired, and you still have the garden to cross.

What garden was she talking about? I could not imagine it; my eyes, dazzled by the abyss's radiance, could not make out anything. In a few seconds, this over-stimulation cleared, and I saw that we were in fact in a fantastical garden where—through crystallisation, metamorphism and vitrification—minerals had attained the most strange and wondrous forms, either by following their splendid whims or by obeying their formative laws unrestrainedly. Here, volcanic action had produced vitreous trees which seemed covered with flowers and fruits made from gemstones, and whose shapes vaguely recalled those of our earthly vegetation. Elsewhere, the gems, crystallised in enormous masses, simulated the appearance of real rocks whose plateaux and summits were adorned with palaces, temples, pavilions, altars, monuments of every kind and of all sizes. From time to time a diamond several metres square, polished by friction with other substances which had disappeared or been transformed, shone out, embedded in the ground like a pool of water turned crimson by the sun. All of this was surprising, grandiose, but inert and mute, and my curiosity was sated in a few moments.

Dear Laura, I told my companion, you promised to take me home, and yet you are showing me a sight which I gave up without regret.

If I had deprived you of it, replied Laura, would you not have reproached me some day? Come, look for the last time upon this world of crystal you wished to conquer, and tell me if it seems worthy of all that you have done to possess it.

This world is beautiful to see, I replied, and it confirms my idea that all is celebration, magic and riches in nature, both beneath a man's feet and above his head. I shall never say, like Walter, that shape and colour mean nothing, and that 'beautiful' is a pointless word; but I was brought up in the fields, Laura: I feel that air and sunshine are the delights of life, and that one's brain atrophies in an enclosed space, no matter how magnificent or colossal that space may be. So I would give all these marvels around us for one ray of morning sunshine and the song of a warbler, or just a grasshopper, in our garden at Fischausen.

Let it be as you wish! said Laura; but listen, my dear Alexis: as I leave the crystal world with you, I sense that I am leaving my glamour there. You have always seen me as tall, beautiful, eloquent, almost magical. In reality, you will find me as I am, small, simple, ignorant, a little middle-class, and singing the *Ballad from Saul* out of key. Outside the crystal, you feel only friendship for me, because you know I am a good nurse, patient with your hallucinations and truly devoted. Will that be sufficient to make you happy, and am I to break off my engagement to Walter who, although he does not love me, accepts me as I am, and asks of a wife only that she should be an inferior being in need of protection? Think of the difficulties, the responsibilities of the role your unequal enthusiasm has assigned to me. Viewed through your magic prism, I am too much; through your disillusioned, tired eyes, I am not enough. You turn me into an angel of light, a pure spirit, and yet I am only a good little woman without pretensions. Think: I would be very unhappy if you forever consigned me either to the firmament or the kitchen. Is there not some boundary possible between these two extremes?

Laura, I replied, you speak with your heart and your reason, and I sense that you embody that boundary between the heaven of ideal love and the respect for reality that constitutes everyday virtue and devotion. I was mad to cleave asunder your dear, generous individuality, your honest self, loving and pure. Forgive me. I was ill, I wrote down my dreams, and I took them seriously. At heart, I was perhaps not absolutely duped by them, for, in the midst of my most fantastical excursions, I always felt that you were near me. Give up Walter, I wish you to, for I know that although he esteems you he does not appreciate your true worth. You deserve to be adored, and I mean to become accustomed to seeing you at once through the enchanted prism and in real life, without one detracting from the other.

So saying, I stood up and saw the vision of the underground world disappear. Before me, through the open door of the house in which I live at Fischausen, I saw the beautiful botanical garden, flooded with June sunshine; a warbler was singing in a *syringa grandiflora*, and my cousin's favourite bullfinch came and perched on my shoulder.

Before walking out of the door, I gave an astonished, fearful glance behind me. I saw the abyss filling with darkness. The electrical radiance was fading away. The colossal gemstones now gave out only a few reddish sparks in the gloom, and I saw something crawling: something formless and bloody which seemed to me to be the mutilated body of Nasias, trying to reassemble itself and stretch out one livid, dismembered hand to hold me back.

My brow was bathed in a cold sweat. Laura mopped it with her perfumed handkerchief, giving me back life and the strength to follow her.

As we crossed the garden, I felt as sprightly and well-rested as if I had not covered eight or ten thousand leagues since the previous day. Laura ushered me into Uncle Tungstenius's drawing room, where I was received with open arms by a good, fat, red-faced man with a pot-belly and the most benevolent of faces.

Embrace my father then, Laura told me, and ask him for my hand.

Your father! I cried, beside myself. Then this is the real Nasias?

Nasias? said the fat man with a laugh. Is that a compliment or a metaphor? I am not erudite; I warn you of that, my dear nephew; but I am a decent man. I have made my little trade honestly in clocks, jewellery and the goldsmith's art. In this way I have earned enough to set up my daughter and give her the husband she loves. I am going to settle in the country house where you were brought up together, and where you will come and see me as often as you can, and every year, I hope, during the holidays. Love me a little, love my daughter a great deal, and call me Papa Christophe, since that is my only and true name. It is less fine-sounding than Nasias perhaps; but I shall not hide from you the fact that I like it better, I don't know why.

I put my arms around this excellent man who accepted me as a son-in-law, young, poor, still without a profession, and, in the first flush of my gratitude, I thought of offering him a diamond as big as my two fists which, before leaving the polar abyss, I had mechanically detached from the rock and put in my pocket. This diamond, of insignificant size compared to the size of the deposit, represented in the world where we live a peerless specimen and an unrivalled fortune. I was so moved, that I could not speak; but I drew this treasure from my pocket and placed it in the hands of my uncle, clasping them with my own, to make him understand that I intended to share everything with him without counting.

What is this? he said.

And, as he opened his hands, I blushed crimson, realising that it was the ball of cut crystal placed as an ornament at the end of the banisters on the stairs in my house.

Do not think him mad, said Laura to her father. This is a symbolic and solemn abjuration of certain fantasies he dearly wishes to sacrifice for me.

So saying, generous Laura took the crystal and shattered it into a thousand pieces against the external support of the casement window. I watched her, and I saw that she was examining me with a certain anxiety.

Laura! I cried, clasping her to my heart, the fateful spell has been destroyed; there is no crystal between us any more, and the true attraction begins. I see you as more beautiful than I ever saw you in dreams, and I sense that henceforth I shall love you with all my being.

My Uncle Tungstenius and Walter soon came to congratulate me on being chosen by Laura, even though she was at that moment engaged to another.

I learned from them that, the previous evening, my sadness had decided my cousin to declare herself, and that, from the first words, she had told her father of her preference for me. Scarcely after his arrival, the good fellow Christophe, actually encountered by me in the mineralogical gallery but so strangely disguised as a Persian in my imagination, had been made aware of the secrets of our hearts. Unaware of what was passing between Laura and him, I had withdrawn, deeply troubled, into my bedroom, where, after vainly trying to calm myself by reading alternately a tale from the Thousand and One Nights and the account of Kane's voyage in the polar seas, I had written under the influence of delirium for several hours. In the morning, Walter and Laura, anxious at the way I had left them the previous evening and about my light which was still burning, had come both alternately and together to call to me and look at me through the glazed panel in my door, which they had finally decided to break in at the moment I heard Nasias falling through the lake of volcanic glass with such a strange and real sound. Walter, who was not at all jealous of Laura's affection for me, had left me alone with her and she had succeeded in gently tearing me away from the hallucination.

On returning to my room, I indeed saw a mass of loose papers on my desk, scrawled on in all directions and scarcely readable at all. I succeeded in putting them in order, and, forcing myself as much as my memory permitted to fill or explain the gaps, I gave them in homage to my dear wife, who sometimes read them with pleasure, excusing my past extravagances in favour of my faithfulness to her image, which I had kept serene and pure right into my dreams.

Married now for two years, I have continued to learn, and I have learned to speak. I am a geology teacher, replacing my Uncle Tungstenius, whose stammer is so much worse that he gave up oral teaching and arranged for me to have his post. In the holidays, we never fail to go, along with him and Walter, to join Uncle Christophe in the country. There, amid the flowers she loves passionately, Laura, who has become a botanist, sometimes asks me with a laugh for details about the flora of the polar island; but she no longer makes war on me over my love for the crystal, since I have learned to see her in it as she is, as henceforth I shall always see her.

Here, M. Hartz closed his manuscript and commented to me:

You will perhaps ask me how, from being a geology teacher, I became a seller of pebbles. That can be summed up in a few words. The reigning Duke of Fischausen, who loved and protected science, found out one fine morning that the most beautiful science was the art of killing animals. His favourites persuaded him that, to be a great prince, a true sovereign, he must spend the greater part of his revenues in feats of hunting. From that moment on, geology, comparative anatomy, physics and chemistry were relegated to the background, and the poor scholars had such slender stipends and such discouraging incentives that it became impossible for us to feed our families. Since my dear Laura, to whom I am planning to introduce you directly, had given me several children, and my father-in-law had made me promise not to let them die of hunger, I had to leave the learned town of Fischausen, which hence-forth resounded to the instructive fanfares of the hunt and the salutary clamour of running hounds. I came and set myself up here, where thanks to good Papa Christophe, I was able to acquire the necessary funds and devote myself to a quite lucrative trade, without giving up my studies and the preoccupations that are still dear to me.

So you see in me a man who has happily rounded the cape of illusions and who will no longer allow himself to be caught in the luxuries of his fantasy, but who is not too angry to have been through that delirious phase where imagination knows no hindrances, and where the poetic sense warms in us the aridity of calculations and the icy terror of vain hypotheses . . .

I had the pleasure of dining with good M. Hartz's divine Laura. There was no longer anything transparent about her: she was a round matron surrounded by very fine children, who had become her only coquetry; but she was extremely intelligent: she had wanted to become educated so as not to be brought down too far from the crystal where her husband had placed her, and, when she spoke, there was a certain sapphire flash in her blue eyes that possessed a great deal of charm and even a little magic.

PUSHKIN PRESS

Pushkin Press was founded in 1997, and publishes novels, essays, memoirs, children's books—everything from timeless classics to the urgent and contemporary.

Our books represent exciting, high-quality writing from around the world: we publish some of the twentieth century's most widely acclaimed, brilliant authors such as Stefan Zweig, Marcel Aymé, Teffi, Antal Szerb, Gaito Gazdanov and Yasushi Inoue, as well as compelling and award-winning contemporary writers, including Andrés Neuman, Edith Pearlman, Eka Kurniawan, Ayelet Gundar-Goshen and Chigozie Obioma.

Pushkin Press publishes the world's best stories, to be read and read again. To discover more, visit www.pushkinpress.com.

THE SPECTRE OF ALEXANDER WOLF
GAITO GAZDANOV

'A mesmerising work of literature' Antony Beevor

SUMMER BEFORE THE DARK
VOLKER WEIDERMANN

'For such a slim book to convey with such poignancy the extinction of a generation of "Great Europeans" is a triumph' *Sunday Telegraph*

MESSAGES FROM A LOST WORLD
STEFAN ZWEIG

'At a time of monetary crisis and political disorder... Zweig's celebration of the brotherhood of peoples reminds us that there is another way' *The Nation*

THE EVENINGS
GERARD REVE

'Not only a masterpiece but a cornerstone manqué of modern European literature' Tim Parks, *Guardian*

BINOCULAR VISION

EDITH PEARLMAN

'A genius of the short story' Mark Lawson, *Guardian*

IN THE BEGINNING WAS THE SEA

TOMÁS GONZÁLEZ

'Smoothly intriguing narrative, with its touches of sinister,
Patricia Highsmith-like menace' *Irish Times*

BEWARE OF PITY

STEFAN ZWEIG

'Zweig's fictional masterpiece' *Guardian*

THE ENCOUNTER

PETRU POPESCU

'A book that suggests new ways of looking at the world
and our place within it' *Sunday Telegraph*

WAKE UP, SIR!

JONATHAN AMES

'The novel is extremely funny but it is also sad and
poignant, and almost incredibly clever' *Guardian*

THE WORLD OF YESTERDAY

STEFAN ZWEIG

'*The World of Yesterday* is one of the greatest memoirs of the twentieth
century, as perfect in its evocation of the world Zweig loved, as it is
in its portrayal of how that world was destroyed' David Hare

WAKING LIONS

AYELET GUNDAR-GOSHEN

'A literary thriller that is used as a vehicle to explore big
moral issues. I loved everything about it' *Daily Mail*

FOR A LITTLE WHILE

RICK BASS

'Bass is, hands down, a master of the short form, creating in a few pages
a natural world of mythic proportions' *New York Times Book Review*